ADVANCE PRAISE

"Corporate hustler and reluctant PI Chuck Restic is back in a new novel that mixes sly humor with taut suspense and an insider's tour of LA. Phillips is an equal-opportunity satirist, gleefully skewing the city's preening billionaires and developers as well as the aspiring classes while spinning a compulsively readable tale of multicultural LA, where everyone's working an angle, connected by hidden motives, schemes, and relationships. A fresh and welcome addition to LA crime fiction."

— Denise Hamilton, author of the
Eve Diamond crime novels and editor of
the Edgar-winning *Los Angeles Noir* anthologies.

PRAISE FOR *THE SILENT SECOND*

"Absorbing.... The insights into the workings of the corporate mind and the machinations of LA real estate are worth the price of admission."   — *Publishers Weekly*

"Compassion blossoms into obsession, turning a corporate middleman into a neophyte sleuth.... Chuck's engaging first-person narrative effectively puts the reader into his unsteady shoes in this promising series kickoff."

— *Kirkus Reviews*

"It's *Chinatown* for the Human Resources Department. Full of humor, outrage, and suspense, Adam Phillips's debut is everything a thriller should be."

— Phoef Sutton, *New York Times*–bestselling author of *Heart Attack and Vine* and *Curious Minds*

"Just when you thought detective fiction had hit a plateau, along comes *The Silent Second*.... This taut, smart, fast-paced thriller is from a fresh author to watch."

— Jim Heimann,
executive editor at Taschen America and author of
Sins of the City and *Los Angeles: Portrait of a City*

"Bodies are piling up. It's the ultimate people problem. This guy in HR can handle it."

— Joe Toplyn, Emmy-winning writer for such shows
as *Monk* and *Late Show with David Letterman*
and author of *Comedy Writing for Late-Night TV*

"Beneath the surface of every corporate drone is a story waiting to be told. Surprising and funny, it turns out this HR professional also makes a damn fine investigator."

— Sarah Cooper, creator of TheCooperReview.com
and author of *100 Tricks to Appear Smart in Meetings*

"The real mystery here is how Phillips keeps elevating the suspense and the humor simultaneously."

— Bob Halloran, author of *White Devil* and
Irish Thunder: The Hard Life and Times of Micky Ward

"Think *Monk* meets *Moonlighting*, with a whole bunch of *The Office* tossed in for good measure—that is, a burned-out HR director who's a hybrid of Marlowe and Michael Scott. Like me, you'll laugh your ass off while immersed in the mystery."

— M. William Phelps,
New York Times–bestselling author of
Dangerous Ground: My Friendship with a Serial Killer

THE PERPETUAL SUMMER

A CHUCK RESTIC MYSTERY

Adam Walker Phillips

PROSPECT
·PARK·
BOOKS

Published by Prospect Park Books
2359 Lincoln Avenue
Altadena, California 91001
www.prospectparkbooks.com

Distributed by Consortium Book Sales & Distribution
www.cbsd.com

Library of Congress Cataloging-in-Publication Data
Names: Phillips, Adam Walker, 1971- author.
Title: The perpetual summer : a Chuck Restic mystery / by Adam Walker
  Phillips.
Description: Altadena, California : Prospect Park Books, [2018] | Series:
  Chuck Restic ; 2
Identifiers: LCCN 2017040168 (print) | LCCN 2017042307 (ebook) |
ISBN 9781945551130 (Ebook) | ISBN 9781945551123 (paperback)
Subjects: LCSH: Murder--Investigation--Fiction. | Private investigators--
Fiction. | BISAC: FICTION / Mystery & Detective / General. | FICTION
/ Humorous. | FICTION / Mystery & Detective / Police Procedural. |
GSAFD: Mystery fiction.
Classification: LCC PS3616.H4475 (ebook) | LCC PS3616.H4475 P47
2018 (print) | DDC 813/.6--dc23
LC record available at https://lccn.loc.gov/2017040168

Cover design by Nancy Nimoy
Book layout and design by Amy Inouye
Printed in the United States of America

Also by Adam Walker Phillips

The Silent Second

For Anthony

THE BIG FLAMEOUT

The collective doubts of millions of corporate cogs were swiftly confirmed during Bob Gershon's retirement party when he summed up his forty-five-year career in three words: "Blah. Blah. Blah."

Up until that point, the party had followed the typical program for a farewell event. About fifty of us from various departments had gathered in the boardroom mid-afternoon, and were treated to a dessert spread fit for a group five times larger than those in attendance. We secretly eyed the pastel macarons and chocolate truffles with gold leaf while pretending to be engrossed in conversations with colleagues, who were also seemingly uninterested in the sweets just an arm's length away. This dance lasted for a few minutes until one brave soul, under the pretext of, "Maybe I'll just get a piece of cantaloupe," made the plunge. The flock took her cue and proceeded with methodical efficiency to graze its way from one end of the table to the other. The only survivor left in its path was an untouched tray of melon.

One of our firm's directors called up the man of

honor. A slightly stooped figure, wearing a suit that was tailored when the frame beneath it was a little more filled out, pulled himself from a conversation and made his way through the crowd. The room broke into applause, and a few folks patted the old man on the back, and with each encouragement the shoulders stooped ever so slightly more, seemingly uncomfortable with the attention showered on them.

The director read aloud from a framed Honorary Proclamation studded with "hereby" and "whereas" and "thereunto." His oratory was interspersed with harassment-proof jokes and served marvelously as a textbook for office humor that was both politically correct and consistently unfunny. The final presentation was of a Tiffany box, and the room collectively took a step forward in anticipation of the contents about to be revealed. It was customary to award associates on their anniversaries with one of those pale blue boxes. And as the years advanced, so did the quality of its contents—a silver pen at five years, a crystal candy dish at fifteen, and so on. Forty-fifth anniversary gifts had a unicorn-like fascination; no one believed they existed but all were open to being disproved.

"Thank you," Bob said with the box in his hands. "I'll open this later at home." The room let out an almost imperceptible moan. Forty-five-year Tiffany treasures were not meant for us mortals.

It was a typical Bob move, one that I had witnessed him perform for as long as I'd been at the firm. My first encounter with the man came early in my career. I found myself in a large meeting on the topic of a benefits program that had gone over budget and failed to show any semblance of a return on investment. My involvement was as the junior HR man who had a small role in the measurement of the program's dismal results. It was getting heated in the room, with recriminations flying. Bob calmly stood up among the fury and asked me to join him outside the conference room. There was a mini-emergency that needed to be addressed, he told the room. I warily listened to him explain what he needed, but it ended up being some random task that could have been done at any time by one of the secretaries. I resented being sent off on such a trivial errand. Only later did I realize that this was Bob's way of saving my career.

Back in the room, the fingers were pointing, and it was only a matter of time before they landed on the guy standing on the lowest rung of the corporate ladder. I never forgot that act of generosity, and when I found myself reporting to him as I had been for the last ten years, I couldn't have been happier. Now, on his retirement day, I was sad to be losing the only man I'd considered a mentor.

"So, I did some math," Bob began, pulling a folded piece of paper from his coat pocket. Putting on his glasses, he read from the sheet: "My forty-five-year career translates into ninety-three thousand, six hundred, and very soon-to-be thirty-six hours of work. In twenty-four-hour increments, that's a total of 3,900 days spent right here in this office. Those good at math can already tell you that comes out to ten and a half years. Think about that—ten straight years of twenty-four-hour days spent in one building."

"Sounds like a prison term!" some jokester felt the need to add. And because of the corporate world's inability to let an obvious joke pass, someone else piled on with, "And two weeks off for good behavior!"

Pausing to let the fake laughter subside, Bob continued. "When I started, we just called it *work*. There was a lot of work to do, and as the years went by, the more work we did." There were a lot of satisfied looks in the room from those who belonged to the self-selected club of the truly hardworking. "But as time progressed, we started referring to this work as *projects*. Eventually, even that word wasn't good enough. It was good enough to build the atom bomb but not sufficient for the kind of work we were doing. Some starry one introduced *initiatives*, and that really took hold. Like a virus, this spawned an inordinate number of new terms, all describing the same thing. Suddenly, we had *key dependencies* and *core deliverables*. There was a period where we even lost track of time, as *future forward* became standard language even though it would take a metaphysics professor to untangle that logic. Someone from a long line of seventeenth-century English surveyors brought us *milestone*. I really liked that one. I personally have passed enough milestones to have circled the earth."

Associates chuckled at the harmless inanity of corporate jargon, but I sensed something darker underneath his words. There was something in his voice and the way it was leading us to an uncertain, but certainly bleak, ending that I didn't want to be around to witness.

"Then militarism came back into fashion, and everything we did was now a *strategy*, and everyone doing it was a *strategic thinker*. You really didn't want to be labeled *tactical*, because that dirty word was relegated to the boys in the trenches who were unable to see five feet in front of them. Soon we had swarms of folks *visioning* our way forward to a place where *synergies* and *parallel paths* would *ladder up* to some corporate Valhalla."

The crowd was starting to splinter among the True Believers and the Doubters. The former smiled obliviously while the latter stared at their shoes.

"Leave it to kids to boil it down for you," Bob continued. "Last week my granddaughter asked me, 'What do you do?' That phrase has become the standard form of identification in contemporary life. It's so ingrained that even children lead with it. Well, I told my granddaughter that I work in Human Resources. But that wasn't enough, because she then innocently asked, 'But what do you *do*?' And I sort of had to think about it for a second."

Finally, we were at the moment in the speech when Bob, the man with double or triple the experience of almost everyone in the room, would impart his wisdom and provide meaning to the lives we lived. It could go several ways.

I help people reach their true potential.

I make sure that we're in a better place than we were yesterday.

I watch over the lifeblood of any corporation—the people.

Bob Gershon went a different route.

"Folks, I couldn't answer her. Forty-five years of work, good old-fashioned hard work, and I couldn't think of a single meaningful thing that I had accomplished. I mean, I worked in 'Human Resources.' It sounds made up, doesn't it?" He laughed but no one joined him. "We've reached a point where we manufacture roles whose sole purpose is to watch over other roles."

In just a few short sentences, Bob Gershon invalidated the daily struggles of everyone in the room. But he did it as I knew Bob would—with dignity.

"Last week," he said, "I came to a startling conclusion. I had a long, successful career but I didn't have a job."

The True Believers bristled at the brazen questioning of their entire belief system. Even the Doubters weren't prepared for this apocalyptic representation of their existence and started to drift out of the room. And I just grew incredibly morose; not for having had to witness the old man's public meltdown, but for acknowledging that I shared his thoughts, often dreamt of this day and doing just what he did, but knowing I could never muster the courage to actually pull it off.

"Why didn't you quit if you hated it so much?" a shrill voice shouted out, but the question seemed directed more at the woman who asked it than at Bob. As if sensing that, Bob waited for her to answer, which she did, internally, and by the resigned look on her face, she apparently came to the same conclusion that he had.

As with all great flameouts, this one ended not in a fireball but in a sputter. "I do appreciate all of this. I hope I imparted...something from the heart..." he said, scanning the room as people left in droves. "Anyway... thank you for coming."

And then it was just the two of us and the crew cleaning up the dishes. Bob gathered his stuff, including the Tiffany box. I brought him his coat.

"Well, that didn't go as I thought it would. I was

hoping to inspire a few people." *By telling them their lives were meaningless*, I thought. The unintentional enormity of his actions hit him at that moment—I saw it in his eyes. "Walk me out?" he asked, more like a plea.

I did just that, in silence.

We waited for a few moments by the elevator banks, and as the elevator chimed, Bob turned to shake my hand.

"Goodbye, Mr. Restic."

There were no empty promises of keeping in touch and meeting for lunch down the road, because we both knew neither would happen. Bob stepped onto the elevator, but before the doors could close, he lunged forward and thrust a purple-veined hand between the sensors. "Chuck!" he called out as he stood in the threshold. I turned back, waiting too much like a young man at his father's deathbed for some last scrap of advice on the life that awaited him. Bob started to say something, thought better of it, and shuffled back into the elevator.

The doors noiselessly closed out his career.

YOUR NAME HERE

I didn't get much of anything done that afternoon. It was hard to concentrate as I replayed in my head the things that Bob had said. It was particularly hard to concentrate with my co-manager Paul Darbin blabbering on about it. Paul was a former hippie who aggressively espoused sustainable living as long as it didn't interfere with the things he enjoyed. He sentenced us to "all-organic" vending machines but God be damned if he'd give up his addiction to chemically enhanced energy drinks.

"What a way to go out," he mused while leaning against the small table in my office. "My big worry is how the group absorbs it. He did, after all, say some pretty poisonous things."

"I think they can handle it, Paul."

"Well, maybe it was a blessing in disguise."

"What do you mean?" I asked, unsure why I even engaged him on the topic. He pounced on my opening and lowered his voice in a conspiratorial tone, even though the door was closed. I'd been feeling that Paul wanted to tell me something and was just waiting for the right opening. I initially thought he was after gauging my interest in Bob's now-empty office with the panoramic view of the San Gabriel Mountains, but he had designs on something much grander.

"Let's be honest, Chuck. The department has been adrift for several years now...." And so the recriminations began while the body was still warm. I wasn't sure if Bob had even made it out of the parking garage yet. "Don't get me wrong. Bob was a visionary. He built this group and did some great things over his time here."

I waited for the "but." Paul cut right to it.

"But every great leader eventually loses touch with the times. Love him to death, but Bob was not up to the challenges we're facing. Adaptation is a healthy and necessary quality for any corporate ecosystem to succeed. And if ever there was a group in need of some transformational change, this is it." Meaningless buzzwords came naturally to Paul. In addition to energy drinks, he was addicted to corporate-management books.

"I mean, look at what we've failed to do on the obesity epidemic." This topic was a cause célèbre that seemed to attract only Paul's attention. He had demonstrated an obsession to eradicate obesity from the firm, a position that went unheeded by our former boss, which in turn drove Paul harder on his mission. "We'll end up paying for that miss," he warned.

"You might be right." I shrugged.

"But you can see where I'm coming from on our group, right?"

"You've brought up some interesting points," I said, deflecting by not directly responding to his question.

Paul was on an obvious fishing expedition to gauge my level of interest in the newly open role as head of the group. There were two clear contenders, assuming the firm didn't look outside for potential candidates, and they both were in the room at that moment. I had zero interest in taking on the enhanced responsibilities of running the entire group, but I would never tell Paul that. I secretly got pleasure from watching him squirm.

"I wonder what Faber thinks of all this," he tried again. Pat Faber was the director overseeing all of us.

"Yeah, I wonder."

"I bet you he sees it our way," he answered. Apparently we were of one frame of mind.

"You never know," I told him.

"What do you think?"

"It's a hard one, Paul."

"If you had to guess?"

"It could go either way."

"But if you were forced to answer?"

"I can see both angles."

This banter played out long past the point where I got amusement out of it. The telephone offered me a convenient excuse to disengage. It was an unknown outside number, but I couldn't resist the temptation to needle Paul one last time.

"It's Pat Faber. I should take this."

"Really? What about?" he sputtered.

I picked up the phone and cupped the mouthpiece. "I guess I'll find out in a minute," I answered and gleefully watched Paul tailspin out of the office. "This is Chuck," I spoke into the phone.

"Mr. Valenti wants to see you," the voice came back. The hair tingled on the back of my neck. I was told an address in Chinatown and then the caller abruptly hung up.

☻   ☻   ☻

The car I'd ordered stopped a block short of the address on Hill Street. If he went any farther, he'd be funneled up on the on-ramp to the 110 Freeway, which led north to Pasadena. I made it the remaining way on foot. The building was literally the last one on the block, where the hum of traffic from above washed down between the buildings.

I recognized Valenti's driver standing on the sidewalk. He wore a black suit with matching tie and mustache. His slicked-back hair, evenly corrugated by the teeth of a plastic comb, was colored with the same black shoe polish as his eyebrows. His gray eyes were the only bit of variation on the ensemble and spoke of his pronounced age. As I approached, I half expected him to introduce himself as the Great Zoltar and pull a set of plastic flowers out of a cane. Instead, he wordlessly pointed me to a nondescript door propped ajar by a stray brick.

The door led to a dingy emergency stairwell. Over the sounds of traffic above, I heard faint voices, and I thought of Valenti as I climbed the stairs. It had been over a year since we last spoke. His actions had set off a chain of events that killed four people. One of them was my friend. Valenti had had no direct involvement in their deaths. He'd had no indirect involvement either. But I still blamed him.

Coming out onto the roof, I was greeted with the sight of the ever-present line of cars on the 110 bending around the hills of Dodger Stadium and descending into downtown Los Angeles. The cars were close enough that I could make eye contact with their drivers. Behind me screeched a high-pitched, slightly accented voice engaged in an impassioned plea.

"You can't just create in a vacuum," said the slender man, motioning to the surrounding neighborhood. "We must take our cues from the beauty that already exists. What I've done is create a sense of space that is true to the cultural and social fabric of this community. It is harmonious with the people who reside here, and that is the great accomplishment."

Valenti let him have his speech, at least for a little while. He brandished the rolled-up architectural drawings and pointed them at the man's chest.

"You have two choices," Valenti responded, calmly. "Your very noble ideals or this commission. I'll wait for your decision."

Valenti left the frustrated architect and walked over toward me by the stairwell. He thanked me for coming and suggested we go across the street to talk. I had no choice but to follow him like a lackey trailing his master.

We made the short walk over to Chung King Road. This was the chop-suey-and-fortune-cookie part of Chinatown, where everything was lit by paper lanterns and where foo dogs outnumbered people two to one. We settled in at an empty bar in one of the older restaurants, which was tucked in an alley. It smelled of sweet-and-sour sauce and ammonia. A surly bartender stared at me with an arched eyebrow. Feeling the need to appear culturally enlightened, I ordered a Tsingtao with the correct pronunciation. Valenti ordered a ginger ale.

"I never touch alcohol before five," he told me as I took my first sip of beer. I was certain that, had I ordered a ginger ale, he would have told me that he never trusted a man who didn't drink before five.

Valenti unfurled a set of architectural plans on the bar and studied them in silence. It felt like a put-on, like he was waiting to be asked about them. I gave him no such satisfaction and let him pretend to pore over the drawings until even he grew tired of the charade.

"It's going to be my legacy," he said flatly.

Why his legacy would reside on a random lot in Chinatown was unclear. He had no cultural connection to this part of the city or the people who lived here. If anything, he was constantly at odds with them. His developments were almost exclusively in the white neighborhoods of Los Angeles or in the pure-white neighborhoods of Orange County.

"What is it?" I asked.

Valenti took a few seconds for dramatic effect.

"The seminal museum of contemporary American art," he answered with a smug look of satisfaction, not so much at the accomplishment of having his own museum, but at the fact that I was interested in hearing about it. "You know I have the largest collection in the world?"

I told him I didn't. He took my answer as an invitation to tell me about it in excruciating detail. His tone shifted to feigned boredom as if he was annoyed that he had to explain it to me. He rattled off names—Diebenkorn, Ruscha, Baldessari—two-thirds of whom I had never heard of, and prattled on about this movement and that school, and only a graduate art-history student could have told you if Valenti knew what he was talking about. Each acquisition followed the same formula—an important piece purchased directly from the influential artist when they were unknown or out of favor or flat broke. He knew exactly what he paid and he knew exactly what it was worth today. His lips glistened as he categorized pieces as "10x" or "100x" or even "1000x," which referred to the level of price appreciation they had garnered since he purchased them. Not once did he talk about a specific piece outside of its monetary value.

Valenti then removed a pen from his jacket pocket and crudely started scribbling on the impeccably rendered drawings. In a few strokes, he added a fourth floor and in big bold letters the words, "VALENTI ART CENTER."

"Subtle," I said.

Valenti looked at me askance but then smiled. "It has to be taller," he told me, "so when all those prigs from Pasadena come downtown for the opera, the first thing they see is my name."

The random building at the far end of Chinatown wasn't so random anymore. It was a lousy spot to put a seminal museum of contemporary American art but it was the ideal spot to tell everyone that you're so rich you can put a seminal museum of contemporary American art wherever the hell you want to.

As a first-generation multi-billionaire, Valenti had the money to elevate himself into the stratosphere of the elite, but he lacked the currency of credibility among that set. Some years ago he realized that fine art was his ticket in and set off on a buying spree unsurpassed by even the city's preeminent museums.

"Well, like you said," I said, smiling and motioning for another beer, "it's all about the art."

This time he laughed.

"I'm worth ten billion dollars, but that means nothing to you. Or it means a lot but you don't want to let me know it."

"The latter," I told him truthfully.

"That's why I trust you. That's why I need you to help me find my granddaughter." I wasn't sure I heard him correctly and looked at the surly bartender as if expecting him to repeat it for me. "She has been missing for four days." Valenti offered no further details. He carefully folded up the drawings.

"Have you called the police?"

He ignored my question.

"One hundred thousand dollars if you can find her," he said and stood up from the bar stool. "Please give me your answer this evening."

He left me with the bill.

On the walk back to the office, I cursed myself for not telling Valenti where he could shove his hundred-thousand-dollar offer. We'd spent the entire time talking about his artwork and the incredible capital gains he'd made off the artists' works, and only at the very end did he get to the real reason for the meeting. He spoke of his missing granddaughter with none of the passion he displayed in the retelling of his art conquests. She sounded like an afterthought, a loose end that needed to be tied. And I hated him at that moment. Not because of his coldness toward a missing human being, but because I didn't decline his offer on the spot.

With distance from the meeting came indignation. And by the time I reached 1st Street, I nobly climbed up on my high horse and worked through the perfect zinger to tell him off. The great one-liners always come much later than when you need them.

But then the wonderfully pragmatic mind took over.

As I began the long ascent up Bunker Hill, an internal pitch session made a very convincing, very one-sided case for taking Valenti up on his offer. Post-divorce, I was cash-strapped and house-poor. My ex-wife got the Benedict Canyon home and half of my retirement. I got an overpriced fixer-upper in Eagle Rock that came with a thirty-year mortgage and no air conditioning during a brutal heat wave. Valenti's hundred-grand cash infusion would solve many of my earthly problems.

Plus, I was bored.

I thought of Bob Gershon and the retirement party and the words he said. We shared a similar view of our roles, and although I was not quite at the point of total despair that he had reached, I was definitely hurtling toward a similar outcome. I could envision myself in that same boardroom in twenty years, giving that same speech.

And it scared me.

By the time I got back to the office, most of the people had left, trying to catch the early trains back to Orange County. I passed by Bob's empty office. You can say this much—the machine certainly was efficient in eradicating cancerous cells from the corporate ecosystem. His office was completely wiped clean, and no trace remained of the man who had given forty-five

years of his life to the company. Except for one thing—
the row of crystal trophies, the culmination of a career,
that spanned the wall-to-wall shelf above his desk. They
were that constant North Star of accomplishment that
I'd gazed at during our weekly touch-base meetings. But
I couldn't figure out why they'd left the awards when
they had clearly gotten rid of everything else, including
the used pencils.

I pulled the desk chair over and climbed up to reach
for one of the statuettes. It was a heavy obelisk with a
granite base. The crystal was a little dusty, but I could
clearly read the etched words next to my fingers:

YOUR NAME HERE

They were all samples from various corporate-
appreciation gift companies, but he'd displayed them
like the trophies of a grand master. Bob said he'd only
recently come to the conclusion that his life spent here
was meaningless. But it was clear he'd come to that conclusion long before then.

ONE CONDITION

There comes a point in life when people simply stop evolving. They settle on the haircut they'll get for the rest of their lives, the wardrobe that will never get updated, the speech that defies the passing eras. The Coverdale Club had reached that point forty years ago.

The paneled dining room was empty on a late Saturday morning except for a few dusty old-timers enjoying the most popular appetizer in the house—double rye Manhattans. Audubon and foxhunting prints decorated the walls and harkened to a simple, bucolic life full of nature and slaughter. A tuxedoed waiter clutching a leather-bound menu padded across the burgundy carpet, but he needn't have gone to the trouble, as I could have guessed the menu's contents without looking: salad of iceberg lettuce wedges and blue cheese dressing, London broil, potatoes dauphine, and thick asparagus with hollandaise, all washed down with a ruby claret.

"Good afternoon," the elderly waiter intoned. "May I inquire as to whose guest you will be today?"

He apparently was familiar enough with the entire

member roster to know that I didn't belong to the club, although that feat wasn't too impressive, since I was the only person under sixty in the entire place. He watched me make one last scan of the dining room.

"Are you meeting a member?" he asked with a growing sense of annoyance.

"Yes," I answered. "Carl Valenti."

The osteoporosis posture suddenly became a little straighter and the voice became a little more helpful. For a name that normally drew my ire, this time it actually felt good to say it. The waiter eagerly led me to a small elevator with another vestige of the past, a human operator. The directory called out the gymnasium, a lyceum for guest speakers, and then "residences" at the top, which was code for rooms to entertain young women on the make. They also served as actual residences for when the young woman got you kicked out of your mansion in San Marino. We got off at the floor with the gym.

The waiter led me into a room lined with mahogany lockers and covered in hunter green carpet that smelled of camphor and foot powder. The room was full of big, white bellies in towels and older black men who waited on them. It evoked an unpleasant "yes'm" era, when African Americans served as the backbone of the service industry in Los Angeles.

I followed my guide into one of the saunas hidden behind a groaning wooden door. Valenti was the only occupant. He sat hunched forward on one of the benches. He had old-man skin, like an over-stretched sweater, with rivulets of sweat running through the folds. The door thudded shut and the waiter left us alone.

"Do you want to talk outside?" I asked. I was already sweating and clearly not dressed for the occasion.

"It's quieter in here."

"Okay," I said. "How should we start?"

"You tell me. You're the investigator."

The man clearly never missed an opportunity to needle.

"No, I'm not an investigator." I loosened the collar of my shirt. "But maybe that's where we should start. Tell me why you didn't hire a real one."

"I've worked with private investigators in the past. They're nothing more than blackmailers in disguise. I can't invite that sort of temptation into this."

"What would they be tempted with, Mr. Valenti?"

He didn't like that question.

"Every family has its unseemly side. Mine is no different. I'd rather not have that be exploited."

"Tell me about your granddaughter."

"There's nothing unseemly about *her*," he snapped.

"I didn't ask for the dirt on her," I said, though now it made me think I should have. "I was just asking for some general information."

Valenti spent the next five minutes describing his grandchild. Jeanette was the daughter of Meredith Schwartzman, Valenti's only child through a second marriage. The girl lived with her mother, who was permanently separated from her husband. He talked about the missing girl like a proud grandfather but relayed the information with a reporter's distance. The words matched but the tone didn't.

I did a stint in recruiting before my current role with the firm. There I developed an invaluable skill called the

Bullshit Detector. Over the last two decades, résumés had become so bloated with fluff and jargon that it became nearly impossible to discern what someone actually did in their past roles.

"Facilitated discussions among teams of senior managers…."

"Liaison for strategic external clients…."

"Workflow oversight of core content deliverables…."

Like those red-lens glasses that kids use to find the secret word, the Bullshit Detector allowed you to see through the spin and get to the heart of what someone actually did.

"Scheduled meetings."

"Answered phones."

"Did nothing."

There was so much nonsense coming out of Valenti's mouth that I had to shut off the detector for fear of it overheating. My head swirled from the maddening array of evasive answers and half-truths. Or it could have been the fact that the room was 180 degrees and I was wearing wool. Thankfully an attendant came in and poured another ladle of water on the hot stones.

"Your granddaughter is sixteen years old. Why didn't you call the police?" I asked.

"There was a time when you could own the police," he lamented, "but now you have to own the union to own the police, and that is too expensive a proposition. They have an insatiable appetite. I don't want the publicity that comes with an official investigation."

"It's your granddaughter," I said flatly.

Valenti didn't appreciate the recrimination in that statement.

"I know it means nothing to you, but that museum means a lot to me." It was the first thing he said that I actually believed. "The building won't go up without a fight. There are a lot of people who would like to see me fail. Do you know about the ballot initiative?"

I remembered reading about a local proposition sponsored by the offspring of one of Chinatown's scions. It was an innocuous-sounding change to a certain cultural heritage provision, which was, in reality, a thinly disguised maneuver to block the construction of Valenti's museum. It was a bit of a local scandal because one of the sponsors of the proposition was none other than the art foundation that Valenti founded and would use to populate the museum itself. Adding to the controversy was the fact that the person leading the charge was the head of the foundation, Valenti's own estranged son-in-law.

"The Barnacle thinks he's so clever," he said, laughing. I assumed he was referring to his former kin. "He still hasn't learned who he is dealing with."

"Is your granddaughter's disappearance somehow connected to the museum?" I wanted to bring us back to the issue at hand.

"That's why I am potentially paying you," he shot back. "To find out." I let him calm down a minute by remaining quiet. He busied himself with the coals and readjusted the plank that kept him from burning his ass on the bench. "There's one other thing. There was a note."

"What kind of note?" I asked.

"An email asking for money." He sounded ashamed.

"From your granddaughter?"

He nodded.

"What did it say?"

"It just asked for money."

"What'd you do?"

"What do you think I did?" he asked back. "I paid it."

"And?"

"And nothing," he concluded.

"How do you know it was legitimate?"

"It was legitimate."

"How can you be sure it wasn't someone posing as your granddaughter?"

"The email came from an account that only Jeanette had access to. I set it up just for her."

"I'd like to see the email."

"I have a copy for you downstairs in the car. There is a full packet there for you to look through." I was curious why he didn't bother to bring it up. "My driver will give you full access to my properties to do whatever you need to do."

"Your driver? I don't understand."

"Hector will take you wherever you need to go."

"I have a car, Mr. Valenti."

"Hector is a condition of the offer," he stated firmly.

"I wasn't aware I needed a chaperone."

"It's not up for negotiation."

☺   ☺   ☺

The front door of the Lincoln was locked and Valenti's driver made no effort to do anything about it, so I settled in on the creaking leather of the backseat. As we pulled out onto Figueroa, I anxiously looked back toward the club and wondered what would become of my car sitting in the garage down below.

"I'm Chuck," I said to the back of the shiny black head.

I got no response.

"You're Hector, right?"

There was no acknowledgment on his end.

"Don't worry, I'm not much of a conversationalist either," I told him and asked that he take me to the girl's home. At least I knew he was listening to me because we banked three lanes over toward the entrance to the 110 south.

I wanted to talk to the girl's family and perhaps look around her house for some insights into why she left. What exactly I was going to look for when I got there was a mystery, but it felt like the correct thing to do. Sitting on the seat next to me was the folder Valenti referenced that contained various bits of information, including the email Valenti received from his granddaughter:

> *Need $45,000. Don't ask why.*
> *Am in trouble. —J*

I had already worked up an unflattering image of Jeanette in my head, and this email confirmed it. I pictured a wild young girl, coming into her own with more money than most would see in a lifetime, living an entitled life of private schools in Beverly Hills and vacation homes that followed the seasons. The ambiguous way Valenti described her led me to believe she had already amassed a cemetery's worth of skeletons that he was both ashamed and frightened of, as they threatened the realization of his museum. I imagined an oversexed waif landing herself in some dire financial

situation that was both inevitable and doomed to be repeated because of the bottomless reserve of funds always there to bail her out. In a very short while I came
to resent this little brat. That is, until I came upon
her photo.

The oversexed waif was actually a frumpy, unassuming girl of sixteen who looked painfully uncomfortable
in her own skin. It was a simple photograph overlooking
the ocean—most likely Hawaii—with a smiling and casually dressed Valenti, his arm draped around Jeanette's
shoulder. Everything about her was embarrassed, as if
the camera lens was the glare of a thousand suns whose
sole purpose was to illuminate all of her faults. She angled her body in a way to spare it the uncompromising
reality of the photograph. She tucked in her chin and offered up a sideways half-smile to hide its imperfections.
With one leg bent behind her, she appeared to be ner-
vously grinding her toes into the sand and would have
crawled into the indentation in the earth if she could.

The Lincoln left the 110 freeway and merged onto
the 405. We headed north a short way, exiting before
we hit the pass. We turned off the main drag and started
weaving our way up into the residential area of Brent-
wood. The houses here weren't audacious but they came
at audacious prices. Many were colonial revivals or ren-
ovated ranches. We stopped in front of a contemporary
structure made of burnished steel, thick panes of glass,
and strategically placed planks of blond wood. The yard
was small and immaculate. Not a single stray leaf blot-
ted the walkway up to the front door.

Hector silently led the way to the entrance. He rang
the doorbell and no more than five seconds passed

before he took out a ring of keys and inserted one into the lock.

"What are you doing?" I asked, dismayed that he felt it was his right to open the door to someone else's home.

"You wanted to see the girl's room," he explained.

"Yes, but we can't just barge into a stranger's house without their knowing."

"This is Mr. Valenti's house," he corrected. "His daughter lives here." The nuance of his answer was telling. I'd watched enough British television series to know that the servants often spoke the language of their bosses.

I trailed him into the foyer. It was an open-concept room with a bank of windows that looked out over the lower half of one of the many canyons in the neighborhood. The furniture looked expensive and uncomfortable. To the left were the kitchen and public areas. To the right looked to be the bedrooms.

"You want to see her room?" he asked and led me that way before waiting for a reply.

"Are you sure this is okay to be snooping around?" I called after him, but he ignored me.

I followed Hector down a hallway lined with artwork but no personal photographs. The other wall was all glass and gave the illusion that you were outside. Several yards away was a stationary lap pool. Somewhere in the white froth was a swimmer beating futilely against a jet-propelled current.

Hector stood outside a door to one of the rooms and gestured inside. Like the guide who brings you to the altar of the holy temple, he was willing to point it out but he was going to let me desecrate it all by myself. I stood outside the room and fought off the feelings of creepiness that came with a middle-aged man skulking around a young teen's bedroom.

A mishmash of pastel purples and greens and frilly pillows, it was smaller than I would have imagined the daughter of the daughter of a billionaire would have. I gingerly stepped into the room and did a quick scan. By the time my eyes got back to the doorway, Hector had disappeared. I wanted to join him.

I didn't know what I was supposed to do. A gnawing regret at having taken the assignment grew into a deeper regret that I was fooling with someone's life. Maybe this was all just a troubled girl going through a difficult stage, but it very well could have been something more serious, and I was playing games purely out of boredom.

A slippery figure in white slid by the door. Seconds later it backed up and paused in the entrance to study the strange man in the young girl's bedroom.

"And you are?" it asked.

The figure was a towel-clad woman with the smoothest, unblemished, most perfectly tanned legs. Her skin had the patina of brass. She was overly toned, bordering on overly muscular. Wednesdays must have been her calf workout days at the gym because the slightest shift on her feet accentuated yet another muscle in the lower half of her legs that I didn't know existed. She crossed her arms over her chest and gazed at me with pale green eyes. A quizzically arched eyebrow left no line on her engineered forehead.

"I was hired to find a missing girl," I answered. That seemed to amuse her.

"Give me a minute, would you?" She smiled and disappeared down the hall.

While I waited, I looked over the room and a shelf piled high with books caught my attention. I always believed the books people displayed said a lot about them, either who they were as a person or who they wanted you to believe they were. Jeanette's shelf had your typical smattering of classics with wrinkle-free spines—no one actually read Dostoyevsky but having him on your shelf at minimum proved that you knew who he was. I also saw an inordinate number of well-handled books with titles that contained some combination of the words "power," "winning," and "transformation." I pulled a few down to inspect the covers. They all followed a familiar formula—an incredibly catchy title with a declarative statement that boldly predicted the simple path to wealth, success, love, or any number of the elusive targets we spend lifetimes chasing.

All the books contained forewords from other self-help authors—the industry was apparently very welcoming to newcomers. It was as if they all understood that a self-help customer is a lifelong customer and that there were enough dollars to feed many mouths. Nothing in their books was actually going to solve whatever problem the person had. But the desire to fix ourselves is an insatiable want and the only answer is more books. Marketers call the path to this enviable position "creating dependency."

There was at least $1,000 worth of improvement books here, all clearly read more than once. Sixteen years old seemed much too young for someone to be overwhelmed with the inevitable existential crisis of adulthood. I felt a pang of sadness at the idea that this girl had somehow skipped the trite saga of a teenage girl and jumped headfirst into grownup malaise.

I thumbed through some of the more worn, dog-eared copies. Entire passages were called out in yellow highlighter. Particular sections were belt-and-suspendered with ink underlines. I read a few of the sections and they were remarkable in how assured the writing was in describing nonsensical concepts. My eye caught a slip of paper protruding from the back. I flipped forward and removed a carefully folded printout of what appeared to be an old newspaper story. I got no further than the date at the top—June 1961—when I heard footsteps approaching. I quickly shoved the paper into my pocket and replaced the book on the shelf.

The woman reappeared in a tennis outfit that was more revealing than the towel. She had taken the time to partly blow-dry her hair, which was now parted with the precision of a laser level. A trace amount of makeup had been applied, as well as a delicate citrusy perfume. She must have read the study about how the smell of grapefruit made people think you were five years younger than your actual age.

"I'm Meredith Valenti," she introduced herself with a hand extended, "the missing girl's mother." There was something snide in the way she said the second part.

"Chuck Restic."

"Dad hates private investigators," she announced and sat down on the edge of the twin bed. "Do you work for the firm?"

"No, I don't."

"You're a *real* private investigator?"

"Define 'real.'"

"Have you ever made a dollar doing that kind of work?"

"No." I got the look reserved for deviled eggs left out too long at the party. "Your father asked me to help locate her."

"Of course he did. Dad always gets serious when money is involved."

"Money doesn't seem to be much of a concern," I informed her. After all, I was being paid double the amount of money that was asked for by the girl I was trying to find.

"You don't know Dad."

Her lack of a pronoun when describing her father was curious. There was something impersonal about it, like she was describing an inanimate object and not the human who shared her blood.

"Has your daughter ever done this before?"

"Done what?"

"Go missing for a period of time."

"Who said she was missing?" she asked.

"You did, when you introduced yourself."

"I was parroting you."

"So you know where she is?" I asked, suddenly confused.

"I didn't say that."

"How long has she been gone?" I tried again.

"I don't know, almost a week."

"When did you last speak to her?"

"I can't remember the exact date. Sometime last weekend."

"Has she tried to make any contact since then?"

"Not that I know of."

She was the only one finding enjoyment from this back-and-forth. I paused and took a moment to study her more closely. She was approaching the half-century mark and fighting it every step of the way. I'd seen this in others—both men and women—who become obsessed with looking better with each passing year in some manic pursuit of a simple phrase: *She looks good for her age.*

Meredith had seemingly reached a point where fitness had taken over her life—a strict regimen of juicing and enemas and twelve hours of Pilates. Yet nothing is as inevitable as the onslaught of age. For every perfectly toned leg, there is a lack of that youthful fat that just can't be replicated in the gym. The response is more toning, even less fat, more muscle, and ultimately two legs with knees resembling giant clamshells. I stared at one of those knees and the leg coquettishly rocking on it.

"Pardon me for being so forward, but you are acting very casual for someone whose teenage daughter has been missing for nearly a week."

"You don't know me," she said icily, "or my family."

"No, I don't know you," I admitted. "But I am trying to locate your daughter and finding out as much information as possible would help me. Has your daughter ever asked for money before?"

"What do you mean?"

"She sent your father an email asking for $45,000."

"Forty-five thousand dollars?" This was new information to her. "Dad paid it?" she asked incredulously.

I told her he had. She got a lot of enjoyment out of that, and the frost that had descended on our conversation started to melt. She went back to bouncing her leg on her knee.

"What did you mean earlier when you said your father gets serious when money is involved? If you didn't know about the 45K, what money were you referring to?"

"There's a lot more money involved than a mere $45,000," she said dreamily. She seemed to get lost in some other thought. I wanted to bring her back to the present.

"Does your daughter keep a diary?"

"Yes, she keeps it next to her favorite locket and dreamy publicity stills of her matinee idols." She couldn't resist. But as if remembering our recent truce, she wiped the smirk from her lips and took a more conciliatory tone. "You don't have kids, do you?"

When I admitted as much, she went on to explain how children didn't keep diaries anymore when they could share all of their darkest, most insignificant thoughts on the internet for everyone to read.

"Where does she keep her computer?"

"If it was here it'd be on her nightstand."

It wasn't.

"And her phone?"

"In her back pocket."

I glanced at the floor by the nightstand. There was a power strip and two empty slots that I assumed were for her chargers. That indicated some element of planning.

"Do you have the names of her friends I could talk to?"

She answered with the names of her friends, not her daughter's.

"Oh, and the Mexican boy," she added. "Nelson something."

"Is that her boyfriend?" I asked.

"No," she said, chuckling, "he's not her boyfriend."

Meredith riffled through the desk drawer and pulled out a photo of Jeanette and a young, dark-skinned boy with foppish hair and chubby cheeks. At least in this photo Jeanette was smiling.

"Can I keep this?" I asked and got a nod of approval. "Is it possible to speak to your husband?"

"Ex-husband," she corrected. "You can speak to him any time you want."

"Anyone else in the house who might have some information that would be useful?"

"Are you asking if there is another man?"

"Actually, I was thinking of a housekeeper."

The frost returned to the room. She bounced to her feet and made for the door. "I have an appointment. Please show yourself out when you are finished."

I pawed around the room a bit more but gave up after not finding anything of much value. I went back down the hall toward the foyer. Hector wasn't there. He was either in the bathroom or perhaps helping himself to whatever was in the fridge.

I heard the key rattle in the door behind me. I first assumed it was Hector. Then, I thought of Jeanette and the fortune of being here when she returned home. I eagerly awaited her and the $100,000 bounty. Neither stepped over the threshold.

It was a man in his thirties, casually dressed in jeans and a flowing shirt open to the chest in order to showcase ten to twenty straggling hairs. He wore an unkempt Van Dyke beard and John Lennon frames. He was as comfortable in the Schwartzman residence as he was in my personal space.

"Welcome," he breathed into my face, "it's good to see you."

"You too," I said, leaning back for a more comfortable distance between us. His breath was slightly sour, like fermented black bread.

"Meredith has spoken a lot about you."

"That's nice of her," although I didn't know how since I had just met her. "All good things, I hope."

"Yes, wonderful things." He had the penetrating stare of a cannibal. I detected an accent but couldn't place it. "We need to set aside some time for just you and me, yes?"

"If you think it's worth it," I replied only because I had no idea what he was talking about. He stared at me far longer than the three seconds allotted for strangers to lock eyes. I badly wanted to crawl out from under his gaze.

"There's something here," he said and pointed to his heart. "Something unique and…powerful. It just needs to be released." I couldn't tell if the power was in his heart or mine. I nodded along with him. "I apologize but I have another session," he said with regret. The calls of a prior commitment broke his fixation on me. His body immediately relaxed and he thankfully took a step back. "But we need time to share."

"I look forward to it," I lied.

He looked very pleased. I anticipated the phase: "My work is done here." Instead I got St. Francis of Assisi with both palms opened toward the heavens.

"With light and love," he bade me goodbye.

"Sure thing," I said and scrambled out of the house.

THE WESTSIDE

I don't know what all the commotion is about," Jeff Schwartzman told me as we crossed the empty reception area in his office. "I spoke to her yesterday."

"You did?"

"She only calls me when she has a fight with her mom." He paused, suddenly realizing something. "She usually stays with me when they fight."

"Do you know where she is now?"

"No, she didn't say and I didn't think to ask her." I watched a growing sense of unease get washed away with a sweeping hand gesture. "She's fine," he told himself. "She's done this before."

"How many times?"

"Too many."

I followed him into a modest office crammed with museum catalogues and art books. The décor was appropriately contemporary with a desk made of glass and chrome, but nothing looked particularly expensive. Conspicuously absent was any form of window with a view to remind you that you were in the expensive section of Wilshire Boulevard. It was not the office you'd expect for the director of a major art foundation.

"Those two are always bickering," he said, sitting behind his desk. He motioned for me to pull a chair over. As I sat down opposite him, I couldn't help but notice the giant black-and-white photograph of a male nude looming over him. The model's instrument, magnified multiple times over, was strategically placed off Jeff's right shoulder. "My wife is not the easiest person to get along with."

"How long have you been separated?"

"Probably a week after we got married," he said, laughing. "Let's just say that kind of money and lifestyle aren't made for guys like you and me." Apparently he missed the memo about my offshore bank accounts. "Look, I married into one of the wealthiest families in Los Angeles but I still drive a Honda," he told me as proof of his humble desires, but it sounded like, if he had a choice, he'd be driving something much more luxurious. "You can take the kid out of Northridge but you can't take Northridge out of the kid."

The kid from the Valley was an appropriately succinct description. Jeff was an unremarkable man in several ways, from his appearance in an off-the-rack collared shirt to his pedestrian personality. I tried to rationalize this image of an ordinary man sitting opposite me and the one of the fitness-obsessed heiress I had met earlier in the day. Theirs was a curious partnership, despite the fact that it may have only existed for a flash. Somewhere in that flash, however, a little girl came into this world.

"You're studying me like you're trying to figure out if it's true."

"What's true, Mr. Schwartzman?"

"All the things the old man said about me." He tried to remain above it all but his insecurity was palpable. "Did he mention the incident in Santa Barbara?" I didn't answer, hoping he would answer for me. "Of course he did. He never misses a chance to bring it up."

"What's your side of it?"

"Let me ask you, is it theft to steal from someone who stole from you first?"

"Maybe not," I replied.

He rambled through a convoluted story about a crooked art dealer and unpaid wages and some minor Impressionist watercolor he'd borrowed as collateral until he got the money owed him. After the fourth time he told me that he was never officially charged with any crime, I decided to put his mind at ease.

"Sounds reasonable to me," I told him.

"Right? Tell that to the old man. You know on my promotion to director, he introduced me as a 'former art thief' who has come a long way. He's a piece of work," he said with a laugh, suddenly more at ease with me, but more importantly with my standing as a member of the commoners. "It's a Mapplethorpe," he told me.

"What is?" I asked.

"The giant naked man behind me," he said thumbing at the photograph. "I apologize. It's hard not to get distracted by it."

I shrugged my shoulders.

"I don't know anything about art," I told him.

"It's junk," he scoffed. Sensing my confusion on why

it was hanging in his office if he had such a low opinion of it, he explained, "Although I am director of the foundation, the old man retains the final say on which pieces go where. This is his idea of a joke. Hilarious, isn't it?" I gave him a look of shared commiseration. "When I courted the local archdiocese in the fight against the museum, he had an icon of Christ smeared in human feces installed in the conference room where we met. Try explaining that to a Cardinal."

He was a broken man who didn't want to admit it; someone who salved his wounds by taking on an air of aloofness to show how little the old man's needling bothered him. He heroically played the part of the soldier in the old movies who tells his buddy he's fine even though everyone around him knows the gut shot is fatal.

"I'll tell you a good one," he said, chuckling. "When it came time for my fortieth birthday, he gave me a thick envelope, letter-sized. In it was a copy of his will." He looked to me for some kind of reaction but got none. "It was his way of telling me that I wasn't in it. What a piece of work, right?" We shared a good laugh. Or, he laughed and I watched him.

"About your daughter," I reminded him.

Again he waved me off and let the laughter draw out to its unnatural conclusion.

"I'll call her this evening and tell her to come home," he said, as if it was as easy as a ten-second phone call.

"Mr. Valenti believes this could be something serious—"

"Uh-huh."

"—enough that he has hired me to find her."

"Look, I don't judge you," he told me magnanimously.

"I appreciate it," I said, although suddenly the tone was no longer among equals.

"You have a living to earn and I don't begrudge it. Heck, I'll even help you get your money. But you don't know the old man. This isn't about my daughter."

"What is it about, then?"

"What it's always about—getting what he wants." Jeff was starting to look a little off-balanced. "He wants this museum," he said with a shrug. "He'll do anything to get it. You can't put anything past him."

The whole thing seemed wildly implausible. But then again this was a wildly implausible family. There was a missing teenager, a worried grandfather with potentially ulterior motives for having her found, and two parents who couldn't be bothered to care.

"Is your daughter close to her grandfather?"

"He's a very persuasive man," he answered.

I got more details from Jeff about his daughter's friends than I got from her mother. I asked him to call me as soon as he heard from Jeanette and I promised to do the same if I learned anything new. He walked me out of the office and felt enough like we were equals to put his arm around me.

"Tell me something," he said, pausing by the receptionist's desk. "Did he use my name when you spoke?"

"Who? Mr. Valenti?"

"Yeah."

"I can't really remember, Mr. Schwartzman."

"You don't have to be polite. I know he called me 'The Barnacle.' It's okay, I like it," he reassured. "It's rather appropriate."

"Why's that?" I asked casually.

"Because it'll take dynamite to get me off this ship," he said defiantly.

Hector was waiting in the downstairs lobby and opened the door for me as I approached. I paused to let a young Asian man coming in the opposite direction go first. Just as the man crossed the threshold I saw Hector flick the door just enough to close the gap between the door and the jam. The move knocked the man off balance, and he stumbled into the lobby.

"Asshole." He sneered at an emotionless Hector.

I looked at Hector, still holding the door open for me, but decided to exit through the other bank.

☼   ☼   ☼

We stopped at a burger place on Pico not far from Jeff's office. We ordered from separate lines and ate at separate tables. He never looked in my direction, but I watched him.

He consumed his meal with the methodical approach of someone who ate for nourishment, not for pleasure. On the surface, he gave off the image of an old man oblivious to all the things going on around him. A screaming baby to his right got not so much as a glance. A homeless man asking for money received even less attention. He ate his entire meal with a dab of mayonnaise on his mustache, a white dot on a black canvas that I could see from a good twenty feet away. Yet all the while I felt like he was watching everything in great detail.

He saw her before I did.

Morgan McIlroy turned her nose up at the modest establishment. She kept both her arms in tight to her body as if letting them wander would expose them to unknown amounts of germs. I looked past her to the parking lot and saw the Mercedes and two girlfriends waiting for her. They wanted no part of the burger place.

Hector led her over to my table and wordlessly asked her to sit. I was worried that our meeting would put her on edge—so worried that I had Jeff call her parents first to provide the introduction. But my concern was unwarranted, because Morgan wasn't bothered in the least. There was an undeserved confidence in the way she casually sat with an adult stranger. She leaned back in the booth and pulled one leg up so her knee could serve as a place to rest her chin. She was around Jeanette's age, maybe a little older, but they couldn't have been more different. She was the oversexed waif I had initially imagined Valenti's granddaughter to be.

"Thanks for meeting with me," I began.

"Sure, but I don't think I can help," she replied. She studied the remains of my half-eaten meal with her lip slightly curled. "I mean, we're not like friends or anything."

"Well, we're just trying to find out as much information as we can. How long have you known her?"

"Maybe five years. Our parents are friends," she added.

Morgan was confirming my suspicions that Jeanette was a lonely kid whose interactions with others came mainly through her family.

"Do you know a boy named Nelson something?"

"Portillo? Yeah, he goes to my school." Then she added, "They give scholarships to families with challenging economic means."

It was a talking point straight out of the school's PR campaign, but despite the altruistic core of the words in the sentence there was still an air of snobbery by the person delivering it.

"So Jeanette and Nelson are friends?"

"Yeah, they're close."

"Are they dating?" I probed.

"I guess so."

"Do you know his number?"

Morgan tapped away on her phone and tracked down his cell. I copied the number down.

"What about a home address?" I asked.

"One of my friends is in art class with him," she explained. "She probably has it," and before she finished the sentence she was sending a text asking for the address. "Jeanette did text me recently," she said almost like an afterthought.

"She did? When?"

"I don't know. About three weeks ago." Morgan again eyed my fries but this time she started eating them. She scowled at the first bite but that didn't stop her from motoring through the rest of them. "She asked for money," said the girl with a mouthful of food.

"Do you still have the text?"

"Yeah." She began scrolling through her old texts. "It was for some sick amount of money, like $30,000 or something." She spent the next five minutes looking for it and handed her phone over to show me.

It was a long text that rambled through a half-apology and then a request for money for something she couldn't say. The amount requested was the same she asked of Valenti by email. I noted the date and time but my memory told me it was shortly after the same request went to her grandfather. There was an address listed where Morgan was to bring the money. I wrote that down and heard Morgan snicker.

"It'd be easier if I just forwarded the text to you."

"I'm the old-fashioned kind," I said. I read through the text a few more times but didn't glean anything more. "It doesn't look like you responded."

"I just ignored it. Too weird."

"Did you ever talk to her about it?"

"I don't think I've seen her since then," she answered.

"Was this normal to you? I mean, had she ever asked you for money before?"

"We never really talked much or hung out."

"Did you ever talk to each other?" I probed.

"Maybe at a Christmas party at my parents' house," she said, then added, "She's just weird."

"We're all weird."

"Not like her. She's sort of a loner."

There was sympathy in her words, a sadness that another human being could be so alone. And there was fear that something like that could happen to her. I started to get a better picture of the girl I was looking for and even of the one in front of me. The latter was full of bluster that projected a confident maturity, but underneath she was very much the opposite. Her phone buzzed and she reflexively picked it up. It was her friend replying with Nelson's address.

"Do you want to write it down?" she smirked.

"Text it to me," I told her.

Before we parted, I asked that she keep our conversation in confidence, but I knew full well that wasn't going to happen. A flurry of gossip among the kids might actually help flush out some more information and it even might help flush out Jeanette herself.

Morgan was back to her casual, confident self, and I was grateful for it. When I wished her goodbye she bounced to her feet and flashed me a peace sign.

"With light and love," she chirped.

☼   ☼   ☼

The house was a mustard-colored box with stucco that was bleached near-white in spots where the sun pounded it relentlessly. The treeless front yard was covered in a layer of brittle crabgrass like hay spread out for a pony-ride stable. An overpowering smell of cat urine baking in the sun tickled the area high up in the nose.

The screen door was intact but the screen was not. I reached through it to knock on the windowless door. A few moments passed before an *abuelita* in a housecoat shuffled to the doorway.

"Hi, we're looking for Nelson," I said in a slow and deliberate manner, but the old woman stared blankly back at me. "Nelson Portillo? Is he home?"

I got no response and looked to Hector to provide some assistance. Instead, he reached past the *abuelita* and pushed the front door open wider and simultaneously stepped into the house.

"Whoa, what are you doing?" I said.

This woke up the *abuelita* and she rattled off a string of invectives at Hector but they fell on deaf ears. I saw movement in the dark area toward the back of the house. Hector saw it too and ran in that direction. There was more shouting inside and then a flash of light of a rear door being opened and the bright sun pouring in.

I stepped off the stoop and ran to the side of the house where a narrow walkway cut through the space between Nelson's house and the neighbor's. I crossed the small backyard, jumped a rusted chain-link fence, and stumbled into the back alley. To the right was a long, empty stretch. To the left was a shorter bit that led to a cross street. I ran in that direction.

Hector stood in the middle of the intersection, his arms hanging by his sides but enough away from his body to be in a pose of provocation. Faced off with him was a young Latino whose age was indeterminate because of his shaved head and tattoos. The young man reached into the pocket of his calf-length shorts and pulled out a knife. He swirled the tip in Hector's direction. The blade glinted brilliantly in the afternoon sun.

I moved a few paces toward them.

"Let's get out of here," I called to Hector. "It's not worth it."

The man facing off with Hector glanced in my direction and then back to his elder combatant.

"Listen to the *guero*, old man," he smirked.

Hector didn't heed his advice. He calmly removed his jacket, folded it once over and laid it on the pavement. When he stood back up, he had a knife of his own. Unlike his foe, Hector held the knife in a fist with the blade pointed down. It felt more menacing.

The closest I had ever been to a knife fight was my high school production of *West Side Story* when I endured two-plus hours of torturous singing because of a crush I had on the girl who played Maria. There was nothing poetic about this back-alley version. There were no hunched-over torsos, no choreographed circling. The younger man puffed out his chest and rolled up onto the balls of his feet in this odd bouncy posture. He feinted toward Hector's shoulder but was surprised, as was I, by the lack of a response from the old man. Hector stood motionless. He somehow knew there was no intention to harm behind the move. What was an attempt to frighten succeeded only in scaring the intimidator.

Hector took a purposeful step forward when a Honda held together by Bondo and duct tape came to a rapid stop on the far corner. Two young Latinos emerged, leaving both front doors open. They instinctively looped around Hector in a sort of pincer move that would have made Rommel proud. The three of them looked at Hector, and then to me, and then calculated their odds. I could see them collectively come to a satisfying conclusion—three against one, fair fight.

But Hector didn't act like the underdog. If anything, he was emboldened by the long odds. He made the first move, and all three men took a synchronized step back. Art sometimes does imitate life. Hector singled out the original fighter and squared off with him. His first step was met with a move that stopped him cold. The young man lifted his XXL white T-shirt and revealed a gun tucked into the elastic waistband of his basketball shorts. The butt of the gun was like an ink stain on his stomach.

I took a step back. Hector didn't move an inch. He stared impassively at the threat. The young man with the gun decided Hector wasn't going to charge him and seemed to relax a bit. He slowly backed up toward the car and his friends moved with him. They all got in and sped off.

"What the hell was that?" I shouted as Hector approached, but he didn't stop to answer. I reached out and grabbed his arm. The old man shot me a look that instantly eased my grip.

"I told him when we meet again I was going to kill him."

"Who?"

Hector thumbed in the direction of the aborted knife fight.

"The boy who took Mr. Valenti's money."

THE GREAT SOCKEYE RUN

First thing Monday morning I called in my assistant, Ms. Terry. She was a 300-pound woman with a hint of an Okie accent that went back two generations. She was full of old-timey phrases that somehow didn't grate on me, most likely because she had the purest heart of anyone I had ever met. I held onto her for a decade despite many efforts to move her somewhere else. In the corporate world, people covet assistants like they covet neighbor's wives.

"Yes, Mr. Restic?" she sang. She insisted on using formal titles despite the fact that we told her not to, and so we added the HR-correct "Ms." before her first name, which pleased her.

"Can you dig up the name of the private investigator we use for background checks on job candidates?"

"Of course," she replied, but I detected a slight hesitation. For the average associate, we employed a standard online service that combed through arrest records and publicly available financial data. But for certain senior roles we needed to look deeper into people's lives.

The public record did not always tell the full story; money and a good lawyer can get a lot of stuff expunged from the book of record. And what's readily available doesn't uncover what we called "soft issues." Mistresses were concerning but not as concerning as multiple divorces. The firm didn't mind people of low morals but it couldn't expose itself to individuals whose poor judgment would cost them gobs of money. Another big red flag was anyone who initiated a lawsuit. If they did it in the past, who was to say they wouldn't do it to us?

My assistant knew we weren't currently searching for a candidate at this level but she was too polite to openly question me on it. She returned a moment later with the contact info for Frank "Badger" Freeley.

It was a self-appointed nickname, but I didn't begrudge him it because it was all part of his brand, to which he remained true. He handled all of our big assignments and he did marvelous work. Most often he'd uncover details that even the candidates had forgotten. I had never met the man in person. All of my interactions with Badger were over the phone, which only added to his mystery.

"There he is!" shouted the voice on the other end of the line. That was Badger's catchphrase, though it didn't necessarily mean he knew who the "he" actually was. It was something he said to everyone.

"Badger," I shouted back, "it's Chuck Restic."

"What do you got for me?"

There was little time for pleasantries with this guy.

"I got a unique one," I told him and then lowered my voice. "But it's not for the company. It's for me."

"Give me the name."

The seriousness in his voice far exceeded whatever assignment I was about to give him. He brought everything to the level of an attempt on the President's life. I loved this guy for it even if it was a put-on. I gave him the name of Valenti's driver.

"Hector Hermosillo."

Badger took down the details I had on the man. I left out, however, the incident with the knives. Badger taught me that part—you want to discover facts but you don't want a filtered set of facts to skew the search for more.

I was anxious to see what he could dig up. Hector was an enigma in this affair of the girl's disappearance. He had an uncommonly intimate relationship with Valenti and the family. He also was not someone you imagined a billionaire would use as his personal driver. The incident with the knife made me think he had other skills to offer.

Hector told me he was the one who delivered the money that Jeanette asked for, but she wasn't the one who picked it up. The young man with the knife was the only person at the meeting point. It was there that Hector handed over the money but with a warning that if he saw him again he would kill him. I had to give Hector some credit for being true to his word. I believed he might have killed that boy if the gun hadn't appeared.

"I'm putting this at the top of my list," Badger announced.

"You don't have to—"

"It's at the top of the list," he stated firmly, "because it needs to be."

"Okay." I smiled. His entire list was filled with number-one priorities. "I appreciate it."

"You'll be hearing from me soon," and he hung up.

With Badger off on his assignment, I turned my attention to the paper I'd found in one of the self-help books in Jeanette's room. It was a photocopy of an old newspaper article from 1961, most likely from its society pages. It was a few-paragraphs story about the divorce of Carl Valenti of Carson and his wife, Sheila Valenti, daughter of Mr. and Mrs. Richard Hawks, also of Carson. They had been married for eight years. It mentioned Valenti's development company, the same one that some years later he would grow into the premier homebuilder in Orange County. It made no mention of children.

I spent the better part of my day playing detective on the internet trying to answer why Jeanette would be so interested in her grandfather's first marriage. That meant skipping out on two touch bases and on a status meeting with my co-manager, Paul. I didn't regret the latter. It spared me from having to endure hearing about yet another solution to the obesity epidemic.

It was fairly easy to track what happened to Valenti after the divorce. He remarried within a year to a younger woman, also from Orange County. They had one child, a little girl they named Meredith. The new Valenti couple became a fixture of the society scene in Southern California and remained so for three decades. Their names were attached to a full book of charitable organizations, saving everything from the South Bay to rescued greyhounds. The second Mrs. Carl Valenti died peacefully in her sleep in 2000 from complications of pneumonia.

Finding out what happened to his first wife, Sheila,

proved a challenge. She and Valenti apparently met at Cal State Fullerton. She was Carl's senior by several years. They married one year after they first met.

Sheila came from an established family in Orange County. There were several mentions of her father and his small manufacturing business in industry publications and business journals. He served on the town council for three terms in the city of Fullerton and was a senior officer in the local Lions Club. Her mother was a prominent figure in the Pioneer Society, a sort of D.A.R. for Californians. All these details portrayed a very comfortable, upper-middle-class life. But there the details fell off. The chroniclers of society life in Los Angeles eradicated Sheila post-divorce.

One thing I found noticeably absent was any mention of Fullerton on the long list of nonprofits and charities with which Valenti was involved. There were at least half a dozen educational foundations and universities that benefited from his largesse. But not Fullerton. An interview with him on his business career made one mention of dropping out of school in his freshman year to pursue a start-up business venture. Sheila was his senior by several years. Perhaps she had completed her degree.

I checked several alumni news publications and eventually found a handful of Fullerton graduates named Sheila. More digging and photo comparisons led me to a Sheila Lansing of Pacoima. Some ten years after her divorce from Valenti, she married Fred Lansing, insurance salesman from Sun Valley. The public narrative for the Lansings was four decades of quiet existence—a fund drive for the local church, a fender bender at the intersection of Alto and Briar, second prize in a chili contest. Fred died in 1998. They had no children.

Sheila's address on Fountain Street in Pacoima hadn't changed in forty years. I decided to make the drive out there to talk to her. I called Hector and told him to meet me in front of my building.

"I'm here," he told me.

"What do you mean?" I asked. I moved to the window and pressed my forehead against the pane. Fifty floors down I could see a black sedan parked in the red zone and the driver standing by the passenger door. "Walk to the front of the car." The figure down below did as I asked. I wondered how long he had been out there. I didn't like the idea of having a driver and really didn't like the feeling that I was being watched. "Okay, I'll come down."

"He that is already corrupt is naturally suspicious," intoned a voice behind me. I slowly turned around to see a smiling Pat Faber sitting on the counter in my office.

"Hey, Pat," I spoke casually. "What brings you here?"

I wasn't sure how long he had been there and how much he had heard. The suspicious comment worried me some but not too much. That was just "Pat being Pat" as people liked to say.

Pat Faber made his reputation on folksy aphorisms. Apparently, he used to vacation in Montana and that credential alone granted him the credibility to spout country pearls like, *"The owl of ignorance lays the egg of pride"* and *"You can't buy the wrench until you know what size pipe you're working with."* They had the resonance of something profound but couldn't stand up to three seconds of reflection. However, that didn't matter as far as his career was concerned. Pat quickly built an image of the "Wise Sage" and he rode it straight to a senior director role. That development would cause much anguish for scores of associates.

It was a firm rite that on every big project someone would recommend you "Run it by Pat." With that single request you were sentenced to hearing another of his homespun summations of your challenges that was either incorrect, incomprehensible, or both. But that's not what you told him. Given Pat's standing at the firm, the responses were much more supportive and included words like "game-changer," "unique perspective," and "out-of-the-box thinking."

Eventually, Pat began to actually believe in the myth of Pat and he became a mockery of himself. It was, after all, a lofty image to uphold, and Pat felt the need to live up to it at all times. The aphorisms fell into overuse; they became hackneyed and tired. The projects associates had to run by Pat soon were of less and less significance. And eventually, Pat just became some weird guy spouting nonsense to the team determining what brand of coffee to serve in the break rooms. This was my direct report.

Pat fittingly chose to sit on the counter and not the formal chair. There was a forced casualness to the decision. "I was up in Washington in May," he began. I pulled a chair up and gave him my full attention. One learned to be wary of "shootin' the breeze" conversations in Corporate America—often those were the most lethal. "You know I have a cabin on the Columbia?" he asked, and my stomach fell out. He was about to give me the salmon story.

"Sockeye are running this week," he started. "The river was just boiling with fish. You don't have to be an angler to land a twenty-pounder, you just need a line and a hook and maybe not even that!"

"That's terrific," I commented but couldn't muster the enthusiasm to match the word "teriffic." "Must have been quite a time."

Pat didn't acknowledge me. There was a story to tell and by god he was going to tell it.

"My last day there I went off the main river and followed one of the feeders deep into the woods. I can't tell you how far I hiked, must have been a few miles. I was exhausted like them sockeye in the river. We were one at that moment."

"I bet," I said.

"Onwards, I continued. And the deeper into the woods I went, the greater the number of sockeye that couldn't make it grew. Remember, these beasts came from Alaska. It was the journey of a lifetime, thousands of miles. You'd see them in the eddies hiding in the shadows of the rocks. You figure they were resting, getting their bearings, but most were just giving up. Some didn't have what it takes to make it. Quitters didn't want to go on and finish the run."

Pat looked up at me, and I knew exactly what he was talking about. The salmon run was his on-the-nose metaphor for our collective corporate careers. We were all on the journey from Alaska to the Puget Sound, into the mouth of the mighty Columbia, ten million strong. Up the river we went, promoting our way from one tributary to the next until the run thinned to just a few, determined sockeye who would finally lay that retirement nest egg that ensures their stock will continue for future generations. Humans have an enduring capacity to attach grand meaning to meaningless things. What Pat neglected to say was that after the salmon lays its egg, it dies before it's able to enjoy it.

Within the narrative of the Great Sockeye Run was a not-so-subtle message questioning my commitment. It was just the nature of things that folks who made it to the finish line naturally believed everyone else sought what they fought so hard to get. And thus the idea that some people didn't want that same glory was wholly un-palatable. Pat looked at me like I was one of those scared quitters circling peacefully in the cool, dark waters of the eddy until the game was over. And he couldn't have been more accurate.

I never wanted the career. This salmon had wanted to turn back at the mouth of the Columbia. But at a cer-tain point it became too late to retrace my steps. A mod-icum of competence had gotten me to a certain level, at which point I pulled off to the side of the great journey and bided my time. The salary wasn't top-tier but it was good enough. And the benefits provided the security blanket everyone longed for. I was safe and out of the spotlight; that is, until Bob Gershon retired.

Suddenly, there was an opening in the department for a senior leader, and they wanted to see if I would go for it. I had no choice.

"I'm glad you stopped by, Pat."

"Oh?"

"This morning I asked my admin to find some time on your calendar," I lied.

"Is that right? What did you want to discuss?"

"Pat," I said, choking down the faint taste of bile in the back of my throat, "I'm the man to run the group."

A MAN AND HIS PIGS

Hector checked his watch with a slightly annoyed look as I approached the Lincoln. I ignored him and gave the address for Sheila Lansing's house in Pacoima.

We pulled onto the 101 and fell into a brisk twenty-mile-per-hour pace. My mind immediately went to the conversation with Pat. Now that I was committed to getting the lead role, I had to actually come up with some ideas to warrant giving it to me. Truth was I was drawing off a barren field.

I focused my efforts on the two great motivators: fear and greed. If I could find one of those things that could either get them to salivate or to soil their shorts, I would have no problem through the interview process. Do both at the same time and they'd be talking about director material. The problem was that there were so few fears left. Most had been eradicated from Corporate America—health issues associated with smoking, threats of lawsuits for discrimination and sexual harassment.

I knew what Paul, the perpetually thin man who never worked out and loathed anyone above a fifteen percent body mass index, would pitch. He'd pimp the noonday run-walks he organized that no one attended, weight-loss seminars that always started out strong but suffered from attrition after only a few days, and one cockamamie idea that associates traveling between one or two floors were required to take the stairs.

In Paul's defense, the medical costs associated with our small number of obese associates far exceeded the combined totals of the rest, and it wasn't even close. But it always felt like there was something more to his fixation on this "terrible disease," something that went far beyond the costs he could save the company. Every new idea was positioned with a false sense of concern—"these poor folks are really struggling and need our help"—that I never believed came from a genuine place. Of course, that could have been because I hadn't had a fresh idea in ten years and was merely envious of the inroads he could potentially make with senior management.

I was so wrapped up in my brainstorm session that I barely noticed we had pulled off the freeway and entered the residential neighborhoods of Pacoima. Hector navigated us through the bedroom community to a quiet street one block from the looming foothills.

The street was in the middle of a wholesale rejuvenation drawing largely off the influx of young professionals new to the home-ownership game. And while its youthful neighbors had fully embraced the home-improvement movement, Sheila's house stood out like a stalwart. It seemed content with its generic concrete driveway and occasionally mowed crabgrass despite the yards around it displaying elaborate designs of river rock, succulents, and PVC fencing.

I rang the bell a few times but got no answer. A nosy neighbor working on a finicky sprinkler head called out to us. He wore an oversized landscaper's hat common among Mexican gardeners, but the person underneath was very white.

"They're not home," he said.

I walked over to the fence that divided the lots.

"Do you know Sheila Lansing?"

"Sheila?" he repeated like the name was foreign to him. "Yeah, I know Sheila. But she doesn't live here anymore. She moved into an elder care home about three years ago. No one takes care of the yard," he said with remorse. "Such a shame. It could be a really nice house."

"You don't happen to know which home?"

He eyed me closely, but he eyed Hector even closer.

"Who are you guys again?" he asked.

I made up some story about a property management company working with Sheila and her estate. We'd worked mostly with her lawyer but he was out of the country and we needed to meet with her about some matters. That lifted his spirits as he envisioned a future where the dump on his right would stop dragging down his property value. He ran inside to get the information I wanted.

"Yard's been a bit of an eyesore for a while now," he said and handed me a slip of paper. "It'd be great for the neighborhood."

☺   ☺   ☺

The Calvary Convalescent Home was a two-story structure that resembled a converted motor inn. It was just
off the 210 Freeway in a semi-commercial area on Foot-
hill Boulevard. We parked under a carport that once
served as a loading zone for vacationers to unpack their
luggage. The air was hot and dusty and recalled the brittle desert winds of autumn.

The lobby was populated with furniture you'd find at
any hospital, dentist office, or clinic—the medical industry had a singular approach to furnishing. Old display
racks that once held pamphlets for local attractions now
contained flyers on estate planning and funeral services.
I approached the front desk where a woman who was
close to becoming a resident herself smiled up at me.

"I'm here to see Sheila Lansing," I informed her.

"Did you have an appointment?" she asked.

I responded that I didn't, that I was a family ac-
quaintance and that if she had the time, I would like to
spend a few minutes with her.

"Don't you worry about that," she smiled. "Our
residents always appreciate a visitor. Any kind." She
called out to an overweight Filipina in maroon scrubs.
"Tala, can you please show these gentlemen to Ms.
Lansing's room?"

I turned to Hector, but he was already headed for
the door and back to his car.

"Well," I said to the attendant, "I guess it's just me."

I followed the woman down a linoleum-lined,
fluorescent-lit hallway. We passed a small chapel where
a pre-dinner service for about five residents and their
attendants was in progress. I tried to make small talk
with the nurse but she wanted no part of it. She silently

led me out to a second-floor balcony that ran the length of the building. Ten or so cushioned glider chairs separated by dusty potted palms looked out on the parking lot below. Straight across was the freeway and its ever-present traffic. If you closed your eyes and thought long enough you might just mistake the sounds of the cars for the lapping waters of the South Bay.

The sun was just creeping over the roofline, and a male attendant lowered blinds before the glare fell on the residents. I followed my escort to the last chair, where a slender woman sat with her hands clasped over her lap. You could see the former beauty under the poorly applied makeup and sweater much too heavy for the temperature outside. I thanked the attendant, but she waddled off without acknowledging it.

"Not the friendly type," I commented.

"Don't mind her. She's just angry that she's fat and doesn't have a man," said the woman and put out her hand. "I'm Sheila Lansing."

"Chuck Restic."

"What can I do for you, Mr. Restic?" she said, wary of a reverse mortgage pitch or some other scam to bleed money out of her.

"I was hired by your ex-husband to help him find his granddaughter," I said.

Her frail hand went limp in mine.

"She's in trouble," she said more as a statement than a question. She seemed to get lost in the thought.

"Do you know her, Mrs. Lansing?"

"Yes," she answered and motioned for me to pull over one of the plastic chairs. "I met her last year."

"How did you meet?"

"Here," she answered. "Right here in this building. She was part of a school program that puts volunteers into the community."

Jeanette's school was some twenty miles from here. There must be a hundred other such convalescent homes between the two. "Us old biddies get lonely and a voice in person, any person, is very welcome."

I glanced down the balcony at the other visitors and wondered how many were family and how many were just strangers trying to do a good deed.

"Did she know who you were when you first met?"

"She said she didn't."

"But you don't believe that," I finished for her.

"No." Sheila unclasped her hands. "She knew but pretended to be surprised. It came up in the most comical way, like bad acting on a soap opera."

"Why do you think she sought you out?"

"Other than our mutual relationships with Carl," she answered, "I can't figure out why."

"What did you talk about?"

"Oh, I don't know. We talked about almost nothing of much significance—things going on in school, some boy she had a crush on, a new movie, kid stuff. We would talk for hours, right here with her in that chair." She reflected on the moment. "All these visitors are here to provide comfort to us buzzards but it always felt like I was the one comforting her."

"Why did you assume Jeanette was in trouble?" I asked.

"Because she's a troubled girl." I gave her time to elaborate. "She doesn't seem like a normal child. There's something very sad about her." I thought of all the self-help books in her room and the photo with Valenti. "I never could figure out why."

"When's the last time you saw her?"

"A few weeks ago," she said, then added, "maybe. My memory isn't as good as it used to be."

I pressed her for details but the only contact information she offered I already had. I found myself asking her more questions even though there was little to gain from them. With rush hour traffic looming, I should have left long before but I had this overwhelming feeling of guilt and found myself lingering. Our conversation wound its way to bits of her life and eventually to her time with Valenti. She spoke of a different man than the one I knew. He came from very humble beginnings in San Pedro, the son of a pig farmer. "He was shy but eager," she recalled. "And the hardest worker I ever met. My father fell for him just as hard as I did, after he got over the fact that he had no money. Carl became the son he never had. My poor dad, he fed us for most of those years." Sheila's father supported them in all facets and even bankrolled many of Valenti's early business ventures, all of which flopped. She spoke of their financial struggles and each recollection tasted a little more sour than the last. She stopped before she got to the part about the divorce.

"Is that hoodlum still following him around?"

"Who's that, Mrs. Lansing?"

"That Chicano character," she replied.

I looked over the edge of the balcony at Hector, who stood by the car in the parking lot below. The late-day sun reflected brilliantly on whatever prodigious amount of product he was using in his hair.

"Did Hector work with Mr. Valenti when you knew him?"

"Inseparable," she scoffed. "Neither of them is any good. Carl's dirty to the core and Hector's the towel he uses to keep his hands clean." Her anger was palpable but it only lasted in that momentary flash. "I apologize. I don't mean to come across as the scorned woman. Carl and I were together briefly but it didn't work out, for no fault of our own. I eventually married a wonderful man who was very good to me," she told me a little too emphatically, as if trying to convince herself of that fact more than anything. I got the sense that poor Mr. Lansing spent thirty years of marriage feeling like number two. I let her drift back into a place where happier memories outnumbered sad ones and then thanked her for her time.

"Will you do me a favor?" she asked as I got up to leave.

"If I can."

"Don't mention me to Carl. And if you have to, don't mention all this to him," she gestured to the shabby surroundings. "I don't hold any resentment but I do still have my pride."

I walked out of the lobby into the sunshine and thought about what the woman had told me. It felt like something was being left unsaid, either deliberately or not.

As I crossed the parking lot toward Hector and the Lincoln, I heard the high-pitched whine of a Japanese compact. I turned to my left. A junky two-door with a cracked windshield was bearing down on me. It was no more than twenty feet away and had no intention of stopping. I heard the car being shifted into a higher gear and I froze. It felt like I was running but my body wasn't moving. The car hiccupped as its operator ground the gears like a driver's education student on his first attempt with a stick shift. The compact hippity-hopped toward me.

The split-second decision was more a five-second deliberation, but I eventually reacted. I dove back toward the lobby even though I could have casually walked over and still made it safely out of the way of the oncoming car. I crumpled onto the asphalt as the car swooshed by, missing me by a wide margin. Pulling myself together, I looked over at Hector. He hadn't moved. He stood there with his arms crossed and a blank stare. I detected a smile.

The shame about how I reacted hurt more than the scrapes on my hands. I was angry at Hector and I was angry at myself. But I was also angry at the person who tried to run me over.

There was no mistaking him. It was the face in the photograph I got from Jeanette's room—Nelson Portillo.

THE PERPETUAL SUMMER

The standstill, rush hour traffic across the Valley granted me sufficient time to process the events of the last few days. One of the few benefits of the relentless traffic in Los Angeles was that it sometimes allotted you the headspace to just think.

I had little hope that a call from Jeanette's father was going to bring her home. The more I learned, the more I felt there was something else driving this saga beyond a mere teenage spat with her parents. A troubled girl sought out a relationship with her grandfather's ex-wife. It was important enough that her boyfriend felt the need to protect it by trying to run me over. And then there was the curious man driving me all over Los Angeles. I concentrated on the black mass that was the back of his head, where even the hairs low on the nape of his neck were dyed. I stared into this void hoping to penetrate the impenetrable but got nothing more than I already knew. He was too comfortable with a knife for my liking and he had a reputation that went back decades. Neither sat well with me.

I pulled my gaze from Hector's head and realized we had exited onto Van Nuys and were heading toward the hills. This was nowhere near where my car was parked at my office downtown.

"Where are we going?" I asked but didn't receive a reply. As we turned onto Mullholland Drive and began the winding path toward Benedict Canyon, the answer became clear. But I wanted Hector to say it. I wanted him to know that I knew where we were going and wasn't happy about being summoned like a bellhop. "Where are we going?" I repeated multiple times like a petulant child until I got the answer I wanted.

"Mr. Valenti wants to see you," he answered dully.

As we passed through the electric gate, I watched groundskeepers taking down dozens of "Vote Yes on 57" placards. Someone apparently wanted to take the message about the museum fight straight to Valenti's door.

The house was as I remembered it. The structure loomed out on the hill's edge. At night, it was an architectural monstrosity. During the day it was just ugly.

Hector parked the sedan on the right edge of the gravel drive and got out. By the way he walked purposefully around the front of the car and into a shaded arbor, it was clear that I was intended to follow him. But I didn't like being led around like a flunky. Even if I was at Valenti's beck and call and slavishly followed the money lurking behind those calls, it didn't mean I had to fully participate.

I remained in the backseat with my arms crossed in childlike defiance. Like other people with no power, I clung to some vague demand for "respect." If only I had chosen a better spot to make my stand. The car's interior

grew increasingly hotter with no air conditioning and
with the black paint absorbing every last ray of the sun's
light. Beads of sweat dotted my forehead and two separate streams trickled down my back and pooled at my
beltline. I began breathing with my mouth open, and
the air was hot going in and hotter coming out. Dignity
came at the cost of heat exhaustion and a dress shirt
stained dark with sweat.

Hector mercifully returned before I required a trip
to the emergency room.

"Please follow me," he grumbled reluctantly.

"Thank you," I said hoarsely, emerging from the swel-
tering car. Before I could get my second foot out, Hector
flicked the door like he was about to slam it closed on
me. He was hoping for a flinch and got a gross overreac-
tion instead. I threw out both arms to stop the door from
crushing me and nearly fell out when it never came.

"Where is he?" I snapped but didn't wait for his answer and stormed off into the arbor.

Valenti sat at a small, wrought iron table with an
ice bucket chilling a bottle of white wine. He flicked
through the *LA Times* and only put it down a good
minute after I had settled into the chair opposite him.

"Why are you wasting time meeting with my ex
-wife?" he began. "I'm not paying you to dig into
my past."

"You haven't paid me anything yet."

He let that one go.

"What led you to seek her out in the first place?"

I told him about the article I'd found in Jeanette's
bedroom and how she and Sheila had been meeting
regularly for a year and a half. I also explained that it

looked like Jeanette had initiated the contact, but for what reason I wasn't sure. Suddenly feeling pressure to explain my lack of progress in locating his granddaughter, I rambled through all the work I had done so far, but Valenti already knew the details.

"If you want more regular reports," I told him, "I am glad to provide them. All you have to do is ask."

"Don't be hurt," he said, picking up on the irritation in my voice. "I demand information on everything I do and get it from any source I can. Do not be annoyed by Hector. He's only doing what I ask of him. He's there to help you."

"Help? Or watch my every move?"

"Maybe both."

"Do you trust this guy?"

"With my life," he stated firmly.

It was clear Hector was giving a blow-by-blow account of the work, or lack thereof, to Valenti. I was curious how detailed those reports were.

"Did he tell you about the encounter with the brother of Jeanette's boyfriend, the one who collected the money?"

"He told me you didn't get your hands dirty," he countered.

"Your 'driver' looks pretty comfortable with a switchblade in his hands. It's a curious trait for someone who just needs to wait outside buildings while you have meetings."

"Yes, he has some rather unique and valuable skills." Valenti folded the newspaper and placed it on the empty seat next to him. The action signified he was finished with the topic of his driver and wanted to move onto something else, the real reason he summoned me to his canyon-top retreat. "What else did my ex-wife have to say?" he asked casually.

"She didn't tell me too much," I replied. I didn't want Valenti to know what she told me about his past but I also didn't want him to think that she told me nothing. He got the message.

"But she told you something."

For one of the few times in the relationship, I felt like I held the trump card. This card featured a young Valenti in overalls picking up table scraps to feed a swine business. I imagined him in the pens with the beasts, stomping through the mud and pig refuse, and having that odor that somehow gets into your skin and can't be washed off with soap no matter how hard you scrub. With his manicured nails and silk ties and perfectly chilled bottles of Sancerre, I was sure it was an image he'd prefer was relegated to the deep recesses of memories euphemistically known as the "early years."

"Of course she told you about the pigs." He smiled.

And the trump card was summarily plucked from my fingers.

"What pigs?" I played dumb, but he saw through it.

"Yes, I see she did. She never understood it. She and that milquetoast Orange County crew never had to taste a struggle." I recalled the dusty balcony at the convalescent home and thought she finally may be tasting that struggle after all, though this one was against the onslaught of old age, and there was no happy ending no matter how long you held out.

"I built this off people's trash," he said, admiring the sweeping views of the canyon and beyond. He was leaving out the three failed business ventures funded by his former father-in-law. Success stories were often written long after the fact. With time, the brain got the distance it needed to self-select the events that led to those grand accomplishments. Distance also allowed one to conveniently forget the numerous failures that somehow didn't quite fit into the narrative.

"Who is the beneficiary of your estate?" I asked brazenly. I wasn't in the mood for an acceptance speech and the details of his estate might play a role in his granddaughter's disappearance.

"That's not any of your concern," he shot back.

"It's okay, I know enough to get the big picture. I know The Barnacle is out and that there will be a foundation for the art. And by the way your daughter spoke, it sounds like she's none too pleased about future finances. Is it all going to your granddaughter?"

Valenti stared at me with a mixture of contempt and admiration; he was impressed that I knew the details about his affairs, but he was angry that I knew so much.

"For a beaten man you have quite a chip on your shoulder."

"You didn't answer my question."

"And I'm not going to."

"Fair enough," I said. "But it might play a role in your granddaughter's disappearance."

He studied the bottle and even spoke directly to it.

"Why do you say that?" he asked softly.

"Doesn't money always play a role?"

He chewed on that. We were finally singing off the same hymnal.

"Jeanette and the museum, of course, are the sole beneficiaries."

"I imagine that at some point your daughter and perhaps others were to receive a share?"

"You are correct in that assumption."

"When did that change?" I asked.

"Recently."

"How recent?"

"Last month," he answered.

That seemed to coincide with the time that Jeanette disappeared.

"Who knew that you changed your will?"

"My former son-in-law." He smiled.

"But he's known he's been out for a while now."

"Correct."

"What about your daughter?"

A long pause.

"Yes."

"And Jeanette?"

He shook his head. It was information that he didn't have to share but felt compelled to.

"May I ask if there was a reason that precipitated the change in beneficiaries?"

"Because I'm trying to break the cycle," he answered mysteriously.

"Which cycle is that?" I probed.

"The cycle of wealth."

"You're going to have to help me out, Mr. Valenti. I am not familiar with that one, for obvious reasons."

"Everything is cyclical," he began, "including wealth. The American fortune undergoes a lifespan very similar to that of the four seasons." The passion with which he elaborated on his theory told me he had spent a good deal of time thinking about it. Spring was apparently the season of accumulation. There, the entrepreneur rose up out of anonymity and amassed a fortune from nothing. He was the risk-taker of a unique sort, for he truly had nothing to lose—monetarily, that is. He risked more fundamental things—ethics, pride, values—in a bid to grow the money at all costs. For a brief moment, I began to sympathize with the old man for no other reason than the fact that he was being honest even with uncompromising details. "I broke many men," he said with neither pleasure nor regret. There was no pretense in the way he described his rise. That's just what one did.

"Summer is why you do this nasty work," he went on. "Your children have been elevated to a social status that you were never able to get. Sure, toward the end I can buy my way into the neighborhoods and country clubs, but to the people there, I'm always the outsider. My children, however, were born into that class," he said with pride. Summer was the full embrace of wealth and all it afforded you. The second generation was catapulted into a world of professionalism and prominence. They became the doctors and lawyers and politicians of our times, influencing society through both work and charity, and still enjoying all the comforts that massive wealth afforded them. "It should go on forever," he declared.

"Why doesn't it?"

"Because the third generation, my children's children, get flabby with the wealth," Valenti scoffed. "They take it for granted. They are too far removed from the actual creation of wealth to see what it took to amass it. And they have that aloofness that comes with entitlement. Environmentalists and social workers and teachers," he rattled off with the disdain reserved for terminal diseases. "They feel the need to pay for the past sins that got them to this spot. But they don't realize that I committed all those sins so they wouldn't have to!"

I could guess wealth's final stage, winter. The fortune has not been tended to for some time. The erosion of capital worsens exponentially and is now hurtling down a certain course, where the only end is some dark and cold day in late February when it's all over. The money is gone and the only thing that remains is the once-glorious name attached to it.

"And they never see it coming," Valenti explained. This self-absorbed generation put half-hearted attempts into careers in screenwriting and poetry. "They're too dumb to see the drama unfolding before their very eyes," said Valenti. "And that's why I changed my will. Because my daughter is doing her damnedest to speed the whole process up. She's already leapfrogged one season and the way she is going, she'll leapfrog two. She always was old for her age," he reflected after a moment's pause, "though she's fighting it every step of the way. Do you know she has two trainers? One for each arm."

He wanted a laugh out of me but got none. Then he seemed to realize the excessive cruelty in his words and took a moment to gather himself. He stared at the sun inching down toward the ocean's horizon. "Jeanette is my last hope."

MORNING LECTURE

I made an appearance at work the following day and popped into a few meetings in the morning just to be seen. On conference calls I was sure to be vocal so everyone knew I was there. And even though being vocal meant parroting what five other people had already said, it was necessary that I do it in order to keep my visibility at a level appropriate for someone about to interview for the role as head of the department.

Echoing other people's thoughts was a tried-and-true strategy in the corporate world. To challenge someone publicly, even if you thought you were right, was always a mistake in this passive-aggressive environment. But to agree with someone, even if you fundamentally disagreed with them, made one many allies.

"I need to jump early," I said to the five people in the room and to several more on the phone, "but before I do, I just want to echo what Bill and Walt have said about keeping the focus on the big picture. I have nothing really to add"—not that anyone would care if

I actually did have something to add—"but I do want to say that I am in full agreement with everything that's been said."

And with that, I rose from the table a good thirty minutes before the meeting was over and, having said nothing at all of any significance, I got the smiling nods of approval from the folks in the room, as if I had just imparted some great scrap of wisdom that would last for generations.

"Thanks for all your help," someone commented without even a trace of sarcasm.

I did have a legitimate conflict that kept me from staying the entire hour. I had an appointment to meet a Mr. Li in Chinatown. The previous evening, Valenti impressed upon me the importance of setting up some time with him, as he was convinced Li had a hand in his granddaughter's disappearance. Exactly what kind of role he played was hazy.

"You can do anything you want," he told me after leading me back to the car to see me off. "You can dig into my past if that makes you feel better. You can talk to any and every one remotely connected to me. But do me one favor—talk to Li first."

I promised him I would. What I didn't promise was that I would do it with Hector. The knife-wielding tattletale was a nuisance and as such, unnecessary to the investigation. I instructed Hector to meet me at the office at eleven but left for the meeting with Li at ten.

☼   ☼   ☼

The sign for the Society for the Preservation of Chinese-American Culture and Heritage wasn't wide enough to hold all the words and had to be laid out in two rows. The narrow storefront masquerading as its headquarters literally sat in the shadow of Valenti's proposed new art museum. The glass display windows were wallpapered in "Yes on 57" posters and created a dizzying collage of red and gold.

I entered the small office and felt like I had stumbled upon a miniature version of the Eighteenth National Conference of the Communist Party of China. The narrow room was lined on each side by about a dozen chairs occupied by middle-aged Asian men wearing near-identical suits and ties. No one said anything but all eyes were on me. At the far end was the unassuming "chairman," who was about half their age and looked like a former skate urchin from Huntington Beach. It was the same man I'd run into outside Jeff Schwartzman's office. He rose from behind a long table to greet me.

"Mr. Restic," he said and pressed his hand into mine. "I'm Gao Li. Thank you for reaching out."

"Well, thank you for meeting me on such short notice."

"Please have a seat," he said and motioned to a chair in front of the long table.

I casually glanced behind me to see if anyone else was going to join, but no one made any such move. I reluctantly took a seat with my back to the rest of the room. What at first resembled a conference now felt more like a tribunal.

I sat down before Li's penetrating gaze. For a man in his late twenties, he exuded a lot of confidence. Li spoke first.

"Mr. Restic, I am a proud man," he began. "And I come from very proud people. Ours is a story of struggle. And Chinatown is the living proof of that struggle." I shifted uncomfortably in the hard chair. One thing the corporate world had taught me was to recognize when a long speech was coming. This one promised to exceed even my worst expectations.

Somewhere around the fifteen-minute mark I added an "I understand" even though I understood very little. They were the words of the village elder in a trite, period-piece movie spoken by an American kid in a baggy sweatshirt. He spoke about present-day Chinatown like it was a cultural jewel of Chinese history. He didn't mention that half the restaurants were Vietnamese and the other half served Chinese food but were owned and operated by Vietnamese. The migration of the Chinese out of Chinatown was decades in the making. Alhambra and Arcadia to the east were where the real Chinese-American community resided.

"But we will never forget the road we've taken to arrive here," he further explained. "Nor the treatment we were subjected to along the way."

I was then forced to listen to the entire history of the Chinese struggle in Southern California culminating in the "holocaust" of 1938, when the city decided to build a train station in Chinatown. To make room for the new structure they "tore at the fabric of the Chinese community" and "ripped families from their homes" and "dropped them in a desolate spot in the city," the current location. Left unsaid in this narrative of Chinese diaspora was the Italian community the Chinese displaced in settling in the new neighborhood. Also left unsaid was the money made during the whole affair by men like Mr. Li's grandfather. Valenti had coached me on this part of the young man's narrative. And although I didn't want to be the old man's pawn in some disagreement between profiteers, I didn't appreciate being spoken to as if I were one of the perpetrators behind said holocaust.

"Was your grandfather active in real estate at that time?" I asked innocently enough. I achieved a cessation of the lecture, but was then subjected to its opposite form of torture—the silent treatment. "I apologize if I offended you," I told the young man.

"*A wise man makes his own decisions*," he lectured. "*An ignorant man follows public opinion.*"

"I beg your pardon?" I snapped.

Li was taking the "village elder" role too far. He could spout Confucian pearls until he was blue in the face but no punk kid was going to call me an idiot to my face. And no one, and I mean no one, was going to trade pithy one-liners with a corporate hack like me and expect to come out on top.

"*It is better to conceal one's knowledge than it is to reveal one's ignorance*," I countered. "And you never answered the question about your grandfather."

From Li spewed forth a litany of threats to me and all white people, threats that were interspersed with hollow excuses that attempted to absolve his bloodline of choices it had had to make. His head was a muddled mess of ancient Chinese philosophy, Marxist slogans, and self-help validations. He was living proof of another gem of the corporate vernacular: he had just enough information to make him dangerous.

"On the phone you mentioned Mr. Valenti suggesting we meet," he said curtly. He was back in his village-elder persona. He seemed able to switch back and forth with ease, perhaps because he didn't realize he was doing it. "Can we jump to the matter at hand?"

"Of course," I answered. But not sure exactly what matter he was referring to, I remained silent.

"Is there a new development that you'd like to discuss?" he asked, trying to tease it out of me.

"Could you be more specific?"

"Is there something we need to discuss regarding our...disagreement with Mr. Valenti?"

And then the roomful of low-level party hacks suddenly made sense—they thought I had come with an offer to negotiate on the museum deal. Given the overall instability of this young man in sneakers, I didn't want to break the bad news to him.

"This is definitely awkward," I told them. "But I don't have an offer."

The gang began to murmur.

"You said you are working for Mr. Valenti," Li tried to clarify.

"Yes, I am but—"

"And that Mr. Valenti suggested we talk."

"—but I am working with him on an entirely different matter. Not the museum."

The murmuring behind me grew louder. Word spread quickly that what was once victory for the cause was not that at all. A couple of them got out of their chairs and spat words at me before shuffling out of the room.

"You can't push us around any longer," Li shouted over them. "While you've gotten fat and lazy with your entitlements, we have risen to our rightful place." He prattled on about the rise of New China and the fall of the West. It was tired prose. But behind it was an anger that went deeper than some riff over racial inequality. "We fucking own San Marino, dude!" he finished with a flourish.

They were the first honest words out of his mouth. And he was right. New Chinese money had poured into the tiny enclave just south of Pasadena, much to the chagrin of the old-wealth residents. In a community that once escorted anyone with a skin shade darker than alabaster to the city limits, the sight of so many Asians gobbling up properties must have made residents' blue blood boil. And made men like Mr. Li extremely happy.

I needed to extricate myself from this situation before it got out of hand. For the first time, I regretted my decision to leave the knife-wielding magician behind. I rose from the chair and faced off with Li.

"Is there any message you would like me to deliver to Mr. Valenti?" I asked with all the formality of a Foreign Service officer.

"Yes," Li stammered, "yes, there is. Tell Mr. Valenti this." Li then pulled out another of his proverbs:

"Man's power is only as strong as what he cherishes most."

As I walked out of the office I couldn't help but think what a curious choice of words given the circumstances. I wondered what Valenti cherished most—his museum or his granddaughter.

☺   ☺   ☺

"Gao?" Claire laughed. "His name is Jimmy."

We met for lunch at a place between our respective offices. It was one of these small-bite restaurants that were all the rage in downtown. It featured two-chew plates that ran upward of fifteen dollars per bite. The casual décor and "hey guys" wait staff were meant to eschew pretense but succeeded in doing the opposite. It was the kind of place my ex-wife loved.

I initially resisted reaching out to Claire. She and I hardly spoke anymore. After the divorce there was some communication, mostly around mundane questions about the sprinklers and forgotten passwords for old accounts. Eventually even those petered out and with them went the last scraps of our relationship and the feeling of being needed. I let her dictate the silence between us, something she was all too willing to oblige. But now I needed her for some information and made the first move and asked her to lunch.

"He was Jimmy for twenty-five years of his life and only recently became Gao," she explained. "He's managing his brand."

"Which brand is that?"

"The kind that caters to new Chinese money."

Claire explained how, after the housing crisis, California was inundated with overseas money, as mostly Chinese investors pounced on attractive buying opportunities to enter the real estate market. For a while it was assumed that every cash offer in the state had its roots in the Far East. "Jimmy—now Gao—got in tight with that investor set."

"Seems like a smart move."

"He's done very well for himself. He has a big house in San Marino."

"Yeah, I heard."

Claire was closely tied into the real estate development world in Southern California. Her law firm specialized in corporate contracts and securitization and her main client was Valenti. Career often came first with Claire.

"How'd you get involved in talking to Jimmy?" she probed.

"Valenti asked me to," I replied.

"He approached you?" She was just as surprised as I was when the old man called me. "What for?"

"He wants help on a private matter."

This about sent her spinning off her chair with curiosity.

"And you accepted it?" she asked with her face buried in the menu. She played it off casually.

"I could use the extra money," I explained.

"You still have it in for him, huh?"

"I could use the extra money," I repeated. I wasn't ready to tell her the real reason Valenti approached me, not because I thought she would use it to her advantage but because I held onto some vague notion of client confidentiality. I steered the conversation back to Li. "What is going on with the museum and this cultural heritage proposition?"

"I'm biased, but it's safe to say that the proposition has nothing to do with protecting some fragile cultural heritage."

Proposition voting was a particularly maddening aspect of California politics. After years of gridlock in Sacramento, citizens began putting propositions on the ballot, which allowed voters to set the course for their state. If approved, the government would have no choice but to abide by them, despite how unfair or fiscally reckless they were. These quickly became the tool of every special interest group within and even outside of California to advance a cause.

I could never decipher what exactly I was voting on with these propositions and thus defaulted to voting no on all of them. I must not have been alone because the writers of these propositions began wording them in a way in which a YES vote was actually a NO vote and vice versa:

Are you in favor of not stopping a halt to the court-ordered decision to cease automatic funding for firefighter relief trusts?

After that, I just stopped voting on them entirely.

"Can you translate for me what this one is about?"

"What they are all about," said Claire. "Money."

The fight apparently wasn't over the museum itself but over the land surrounding the museum. Cultural hotspots were all the rage in the downtown revitalization push and a boon to developers of high-end condos.

"Who owns the land around the museum?" I asked naively. Claire's smile gave me my answer. "And Gao wants a piece?"

"It's a brand thing," she explained. "He wants to be the go-to man for foreign investors. A development in his backyard without him having a piece is a blow to his image," she said. "The Chinese are very proud. He doesn't want to lose face."

"Is the proposition going to pass?"

"That's the hard part about propositions—the outcomes are almost entirely random."

"How nervous is the Valenti camp?"

"It's nothing that can't be overturned at a later date."

"But that would take a lot of time and a lot of money," I added.

"And Carl isn't the patient type."

Shop talk ended once the food arrived. Career might have been a priority for Claire, but dining out was her real love.

"You have to try these *arrancini*," she gushed and held a plate out for me. "We had it last week and it was amazing."

"How is Mr. Teeth?" I asked casually. "Is he still trying to open a regatta on the LA River?"

Claire humored me with a smile. Her boyfriend was a square-jawed square and product of some English-sounding East Coast prep school. He could boil water and somehow make you feel inferior.

"Todd and I are just friends."

"Sorry, I didn't know," I said.

"Don't go feeling sorry for me," she shot back. "I met someone else. He's got a great mind and a passion for what he does." The latter was definitely a shot in my direction. "He owns an art gallery down the road and he's doing really well. He was just featured in a *Times* piece about Next Gen galleries. He reps some big names and has some pretty amazing stuff."

"His family is wealthy?" I asked.

"Why do you say that?"

"Because no one owns a gallery and actually makes money off it."

That hurt her more than I intended.

"You must be alone," she surmised. "Otherwise

you wouldn't be so interested, and nasty about what I have going on." That pretty much soured the rest of the lunch. I tried several times to right the ship but all my attempts fell flat.

"I'm sorry for being a jerk," I said.

Claire didn't acknowledge it right away. She waited until we had finished the meal and drifted out onto the sidewalk crammed with office workers returning from their lunch hour. She gave me a friends-only hug and whispered in my ear:

"Get yourself a girl, Chuck."

☀   ☀   ☀

When I got back to the office, Ms. Terry was waiting for me by the entrance to our floor. She looked anxious and when I inquired as to why she was hanging by the door, she leaned in to whisper.

"Mr. Restic, you have a visitor."

I looked over her shoulder at the reception area. Hector was sitting on one of the leather couches and impassively watching a video extolling our corporate values that played on loop all day. It drove anyone within earshot to near-insanity but it looked like Hector was hypnotized by it.

"Don't worry, he can wait a little longer," I told her and headed toward my office before Hector saw me.

"But Mr. Restic, he said it was quite important that he speak to you. He'll be out of the restroom shortly," she explained.

"Restroom? Who are you talking about?"

"Sorry about that," a voice boomed behind me. "Bacon hot dog didn't sit right with me."

Detective Ricohr waddled his way toward us. His voice brought Hector out of his hypnotic state, and he too came in my direction. The four of us stood there staring at each other. I spoke first.

"What brings you here, detective?" I asked.

Hector pivoted, pulling a banking maneuver straight out of the Blue Angels playbook. He quickly retreated out the glass doors toward the elevators.

"I didn't catch your name," Detective Ricohr called out after him.

"Hector," the old magician shot back.

"Hector what?"

"Just Hector," he answered and disappeared into the elevator car.

"Just Hector," the detective laughed.

I gestured empathetically to his area of suffering. "I see your feet are still bothering you."

"And I thought I was getting better," he replied and looked around. "Should we go to your office?"

"We should be good here," I replied.

Ms. Terry didn't want to intrude and excused herself. She wasn't more than a few feet away when Detective Ricohr threw out his first question.

"So what do you know about Jeanette Schwartzman?"

It was a cheap tactic to get a visceral reaction from me. I was familiar enough with the detective to not fall for it.

"I know of her," I answered, "but I have never met her."

"Carl Valenti's granddaughter, right?"

"That's correct."

"I didn't think you liked that man," he said.

Detective Ricohr was well aware of my feelings toward Valenti. He investigated the murder of my friend, a murder that I believed Valenti was connected to. It turned out not to be true, but that didn't completely absolve him.

"I don't like him," I answered.

"But things change," he finished for me. "Want to fill me in on what that could be?"

"I'm helping him with a personal matter. With his granddaughter."

"When's the last time you spoke to her?" he asked.

"I haven't."

"So she's missing. That's interesting." He wrote something in his notepad that took far longer to write than anything I had yet told him. "We found your number on a cell phone belonging to a murder victim—Morgan McIlroy. Young girl, blond?"

It took a moment for it to register. And when it finally did it was like the oxygen was being pulled from my lungs. I think I might have taken a slight step backward.

"You're not going to faint, are you?"

"I know Morgan. I mean, I met her once," I felt the need to clarify not because I wanted to avoid suspicion but because there was a sudden distance between me and the young girl that somehow warranted an impersonal tone. Detective Ricohr continued with the theme of detachment.

"She was strangled, dumped in a car in a parking lot in Chinatown. We're checking security cameras to see if we can get a shot of the killer," he added matter-of-factly.

I recalled my encounter with the precocious girl at the burger stand. Only when I summoned an image of the young girl—sitting there in the booth eating my fries and doing her best to answer my questions—did it finally strike me that she was dead.

"Jesus," I breathed. "We just met the other day."

"Want to fill me in on what you talked about?"

I hesitated.

"It was in reference to the other thing I talked about with Valenti. But I shouldn't say anything more until I can talk to the family."

"It sounds like they could be connected."

"I wouldn't want to speculate," I said.

"Of course you wouldn't," he responded. As he turned to leave he requested that I call him as soon as I talked to the old man. And he had some unsolicited advice for me.

"If you didn't trust him before, I don't know why you would trust him now."

HIGH NOON

"There he is!" he shouted as I entered.

Badger's office was half of the ground floor of a three-story apartment building located on a side street in Echo Park. The only evidence that it was an actual office was a handwritten sign on poster board pasted in the upper corner of the large picture window facing the sidewalk.

I got the call from Badger Thursday afternoon, which left me barely enough time to plant the seed of a "tickle" in the back of my throat that invariably would develop into a full-blown sore throat later that night. I heroically answered a few emails on Friday morning and then sent word around that I was going to stay home to rest. "There goes my weekend!" I lamented and successfully cleared the day to meet Badger in person.

The carpet in his office was a deep gold made deeper by the years of foot traffic from shoes comfortable walking on dusty streets. Its edges didn't cleanly fit with the wall and was probably a cast-off from another office undergoing an update. There was little furniture outside of a desk, filing cabinet, and a bookcase that looked like surplus from a 1970s schoolroom. I didn't spot a computer. The only attempt at decoration was a cloudy vase of dried pussy willows and a borrowed frame displaying Badger's private investigator credentials.

The one question that sprang to mind as I took in the surroundings, a question that I needed to address as soon as I got back to the office, was *who the hell did the background check on the background checker?*

"Chuck," he said, rising from his desk, "good to finally meet you in person."

Badger was one of those guys who tucked his sweater into his jeans and didn't wear a belt. He had a handshake that could crack walnuts and his skin was about as rough as the broken shells. His hair was the color and texture of dirty straw and I couldn't tell if all of it was real.

"Thanks for making this a priority," I told him and took a seat in a creaky chair. Behind Badger's desk, a makeshift wall and curtained doorway separated the front of the office from a back room. Over his shoulder and through the slat in the curtain, I spotted an Army cot, mini-fridge, and hotplate. This was what savvy real estate agents would deem a "mixed-use" space.

"You'll always be the priority," he told me. I pitied the utterly unimportant person who wasn't the recipient of this phrase because, as far as I could tell, he said it to everyone.

"I found some things," he stated firmly. "Let us begin."

I marveled at the lack of paper in the entire exchange. The only sign of paper anywhere in the office was a yellow newspaper on his desk that looked a decade from being current. If this was a corporate meeting, he'd have a thirty-five-page flipbook with the first third filled with table of contents, title dividers, biographies of the participants, and other such nonsense. There would also be an appendix that you would be instructed to "read at your leisure." Somewhere in the middle of this mess would be the actual meat of the presentation that could be boiled down to a few, succinct bullets. The only way to hear them was to endure a long presentation by the person who put it together. That was why every meeting in corporate America is at least one hour long. Badger wouldn't make it in that world.

"In 1963 Hector Hermosillo was arrested and charged with the stabbing death of a teenager in the Alpine district. He was twenty-two at the time. The police arrested him at the scene without incident."

"Knife fight," I repeated.

"One of them had a knife, anyway. The police put it down as a racial dispute, perhaps gang related. There was concern that it could boil over to another race riot and put a lot of men on the streets."

Los Angeles at that time was a bit of a powder keg as the city was beginning to resemble the ethnically diverse mishmash that it is today. Friction between the various groups—blacks, Mexicans, Japanese, whites, Chinese—jostling for space and jobs and respect sometimes flared up into full-on melees. These resulted in many deaths but never much will to change the things that led to them.

"Latino was one group. Who was the other?" I asked even though I could have guessed.

"Chinese," he confirmed.

"Where's the Alpine district? I've never heard of that."

"It's those little hills between Chinatown and the south side of Dodger Stadium. Used to be mostly an Italian neighborhood until the Chinese moved in. You still have a few decent Italian delis there left over from the old days."

"You mentioned a gang?"

"This is where it gets complicated. Mr. Hermosillo was one of these *pachuco* wannabe punks from East LA. White Picket guy, maybe, but never confirmed if he was officially a member."

No wonder Hector wore his pants so high. The original Chicano gangs were the zoot-suited playboys of the streets. They wore sports coats to their knees and pants to their chests.

"He was in a gang, huh?"

"There's mention of it in the original police report but, like I said, it was unconfirmed."

I wondered how he got access to this level of information. He must have an inside source at the department but I don't believe he was ever employed by them. I made a second mental note to run a background check on him.

"Was the victim in a gang?" I asked.

"Not sure."

"Did he have a personal connection to Hector?"

"You're asking the wrong questions, guy."

Badger was one of the few men to call other men "guy" and not have it come off as an invitation to a fight. There was an excitement in his voice as if he had some bit of information that he wanted me to discover. But it bristled all the same. I prided myself on having a first-rate interviewing skill set, which included asking the right questions at the right time. The direct challenge to my ability to ask pertinent questions was an open-handed slap to my corporate face.

"Were the Chicano gangs active in the Alpine district at that time?" I asked after giving it more thought.

"You're getting warmer."

"Did Hector serve time for the murder?"

"Much warmer."

"Was he even convicted?"

"He was not."

"Why?"

"Because an eyewitness confirmed that his actions were in self-defense."

"One of his friends vouched for him and they dropped the charges?" I asked incredulously.

"A very well-respected, upstanding friend." He smiled.

"Valenti?"

And the smile that was partially concealed during this excruciating game of twenty questions finally emerged in all of its yellowed brilliance.

My mind raced with the permutations of what this development meant in the already-complex nest of relationships around the disappearance of a young girl. The loyal driver of thirty years owed both his livelihood and his life to the man who employed him. Or was it reversed? Was the job payback for a sordid deed in the Alpine district in the early 1960s?

"I did a little more digging on the murder. No charge, of course, this is just Badger being Badger. It's who I am and it's what I do. I get on something and I can't let it go until I know everything about it. Must be in my blood—"

"What did you find out?" I interrupted before he launched into a family tree discussion about being a direct descendent of a long line of Nez Perce Indian trackers.

"The victim? He wasn't a nameless punk from the neighborhood. He came from an influential Chinese family with a lot of money. They did most of the developments in the area, including the ones in Alpine."

"Last name was Li," I said for him.

"With an 'I.' How did you know?" he asked, surprised.

"I had a feeling."

"Maybe you have some Cherokee in you, too," he said, laughing.

The fun and games were short-lived.

"We got an issue," Badger whispered. He slowly moved the folded, yellow newspaper that was on the desk and placed it in front of me. I picked it up and scanned the page.

"I don't see it," I said. "Is there a story about Valenti in here?"

"Behind you," Badger said softly.

I followed Badger's gaze and spun around in my chair and got a look at what was distressing him. Through the arrangement of dried pussy willows that stood in front of the large picture window, I could make out the face of Hector Hermosillo, his hands cupped on the glass to peer in beyond the glare.

"Jesus, how did he get here?"

"Do we have a situation?" Badger asked gravely.

"No, I don't think so—"

Turning back, I noticed the gun in Badger's hand and realized it had been hidden under the newspaper the entire time. I made a mental note to add the letters "ASAP" next to the background check we needed to run on Badger.

"What's the score, guy?"

"There's no score," I said. "Let me handle this."

I walked out to the street and faced off with Hector.

"What are you doing here?"

"We were supposed to meet this morning," he answered mechanically.

"Yeah, well, my plans changed. Why are you following me?"

"We were supposed to meet this morning," he repeated.

"You already said that. Listen, I didn't sign up for this job to be tailed like a common criminal. That was not part of the bargain. I will let you know when and where I need your help and you will not question me when plans change. You need to understand your place and do as you are instructed."

It was a dressing-down straight out of an English manor television series. It was full of indignation and pompous self-righteousness. And it was wholly ignored by my *pachuco* friend.

"Who's he?" he motioned to Badger's office. Glancing in, I realized Badger himself was no longer in there.

"This is my personal business."

I watched Hector read the sign announcing Badger's trade. He looked at me like someone who had double-crossed him. Or like someone who caught his spouse cheating. Anger and disappointment were a deadly combination.

"I'm making progress," I felt the need to justify. "If your boss wants regular updates, all he has to do ask. I don't need an intermediary, let alone one who makes me feel like I am the one under investigation."

But what I really wanted was to avoid having Hector tell Valenti that I engaged the services of a private investigator. Valenti's mistrust toward the profession—in this case, seemingly justified—might very well get me dismissed from the job. And when I glanced across the street, my potential termination seemed more likely.

Badger stood next to a parked car, his eyes hidden behind very large, very dark sunglasses. One hand casually held the yellow newspaper in front of his belt. The other hand held something heavy behind it.

I had nightmarish images of a knife and gun battle in the sun-drenched streets of midday Los Angeles and having to explain it all to the police, to Valenti, and to work. I moved around to step in between Badger and his direct line on Hector before anything happened. I then filled Hector in on the progress I had made that morning with Gao. I instructed him to pass this information along to Mr. Valenti.

"We got an issue here?" interrupted a voice behind me.

Badger stood off my left shoulder and although he was speaking to me, he stared only at Hector.

"There is no problem," I answered.

"Unfortunately, it looks like there is," he warned. "*Traendo cola, ruco.*" It sounded like pigeon Spanish. "Yeah, I speak *calo.*"

Hector slowly put his hand inside his pants pocket. Badger responded by moving aside the newspaper to reveal the gun. He cocked the hammer with his thumb.

"*Filero* versus a *fusca*," Badger said. "Bad odds for you, *negrita linda*."

I'd seen this movie once before and knew the flash of a gun wasn't enough to scare Hector off. But to my surprise and great relief, the old magician slowly retreated and returned to his car. We watched him drive off down the road.

I had successfully averted one disaster but now had another on my hands. If an alleged murderer who just the other day wasn't scared of three punks with knives and guns backed down from a fight with far better odds, what did that say about my private investigator?

I made a fourth mental note to terminate all relationships with Badger and his firm, effective immediately.

☀   ☀   ☀

It was one of the few historic homes on the Alhambra street to survive the onslaught of 1950s two-story commercial real estate construction, but it didn't come out of that battle unscathed. The gabled front rising among the near perfectly leveled rooflines beside it seemed dangerously close to toppling over. Its porch was ripped away, exposing an underbelly not worthy of a street-facing view.

I parked in front of an *agua fresca*, a type of store that caters to the suspicions of newly arrived immigrants about the potability of tap water. The store was a maze of tubes and filters and tanks designed to make it look scientific, when beneath all of the tubes and filters and tanks was the same source of water the customers were lining up to avoid in the first place. A worker out front hosed off the sidewalk, and I half-wanted to ask if he was using filtered water.

I checked the address of the dilapidated home across the street with the one I had written down from the text Jeanette had sent Morgan. In it, she was instructed to bring the money to this place. My mind ran through the possibilities of what I was going to find as I jaywalked across the street. The block was one of those unshaded streets on which the summer sun and concrete had long ago vanquished any and all of its leafy companions. Waves of heat radiated up and softened my rubber soles, making it feel like I was wearing cushioned inserts.

I knocked on the metal-gated front door and got no response. I rattled the door long enough to call the attention of a woman inside. To say she was expressionless wasn't fair to the millions of people who actually were. She almost had a negative energy, like a black hole that sucked emotion from anyone around her.

"Hi," I said to the impassive face. She was Asian, somewhere in her fifties. It wasn't clear if she even understood my first line. "I'm wondering if you can help me. I'm looking for a friend of mine. I think she might be here."

I rambled on like that for a while when her face suddenly broke into a wide smile. I tried to think what it was I said that got the reaction but then realized it had nothing to do with me but with what was behind me. A small Asian family laden with balloons and trays of food and bags of presents approached. The parents were smiling. The children were glum. They looked like they were on their way to church.

The gatekeeper gently brushed me aside to allow room for the family to pass. They were warmly welcomed into the home in a language I didn't understand. I tried to catch a glimpse of what was just beyond the door but it was too dark to see much of what was inside and the metal grate was quickly shut in my face. I tried knocking again but my attempt yielded no results.

I returned to my car across the street.

"Crazy people," commented the man watering the sidewalk. "You going to shut them down?"

"I might," I said, not sure what specifically he wanted me to close but very curious to find out. "What's the deal over there?"

"In and out, all day. They take up all the parking," he said with annoyance, waving his hand, and the hose with it, at the surrounding street. I had to jump back to avoid getting splashed with the water.

"What business are they running out of there?"

"You from the city?" he asked, now unsure who I was. Alhambra may have gone Latino, then Asian years ago, but the race of the elected officials had yet to catch up. White men in this town meant cops or city council.

"Sure," I replied without a trace of conviction, "I'm from the city." I even cinched up my pants in a futile attempt to convey a position of authority. The man watering the sidewalk didn't buy it. He stared at me as precious gallons of water flowed into the storm drain. I gestured to the water. "Do you mind shutting that off so we can talk?"

He was polite enough to wait two seconds before simply turning his back on me to continue on with his business. It was then that I noticed the black sedan parked a ways down the street. I couldn't see into the driver's window because of the glare on the glass, but I knew the car and I knew the operator.

So Valenti's driver was now tailing me around the city. Part of me wanted to confront him and end this dance once and for all. And then part of me wanted to leave Hector in that car as I pretended to paw around the neighborhood shops. It was nearing ninety-five degrees and with no shade, it felt even hotter. I wanted to sweat him out. I decided instead to lose him for good.

My home was to the north, but I didn't want to lead Hector to it. So I went east on the 10 Freeway. I got off at a random exit and as I rolled down the off-ramp, I glanced in my mirror and saw the black sedan settling in a few cars behind me. I turned right onto the boulevard and went a few blocks before turning off onto one of the smaller streets. I led Hector on a series of alternating turns but I couldn't seem to lose him. I pulled into a mini–shopping mall and tried to shake him in an underground parking lot but there were too many cars. We ended up in an awkward moment of being bumper-to-bumper while a shopper took forever to back out of her parking space. I stared at Hector in the rearview mirror. He stared back, his expression obscured by sunglasses. I gave him a quick wave.

Back on the boulevard, I decided I had had enough and with the light already yellow and my car a good fifteen feet from the intersection, I floored it and lurched out just as the light turned red. I looked back and saw

Hector stopped behind the car that separated us, and a big smile crossed my lips at the pure satisfaction of having slipped his tail. This big, beautiful smile was later framed up nicely by the traffic camera that caught me running the red and mailed me the photo along with a $300 ticket.

I had dinner at a random taco stand and leisurely made my way using surface streets back to Eagle Rock. By the time I arrived in my neighborhood, the sun had slipped below the horizon and ended yet another mercilessly hot day. I pulled onto my street off Colorado and as I approached my house I noticed the black sedan parked in front of it. The driver's window was down. Hector had the seat titled back and dozed casually in the cooling evening air.

I leaned on the horn three seconds longer than necessary as I pulled into my garage and huffily made my way into the house. The place was stuffy and had a faint trace of grapefruit.

"You need central air," a voice called out from the darkness.

NEW HIRE

Meredith Valenti sat on the leather sofa. Her overly tanned legs showed little contrast to the chocolate-colored couch but the electric green dress certainly did. It was a one-piece halter dress, and it represented the only splash of color in the room.

"I'm sticking," she complained and stood up to a tearing sound as her skin pulled away from the leather. The dress, whose hemline was high on her thigh when seated, didn't come down much now that she was standing. She looked about the sparsely furnished room with casual interest.

"Do you have anything to drink?" she asked, more like she was addressing the maid than someone whose house she had broken into. I ignored her request and asked why she was there. She in turn ignored my question and asked me a new one.

"Do you know why I dress like this?"

"I have no idea," I told her.

"Because I can."

"Seems like a good enough reason for me."

"How old do you think I am?"

"Fifty-nine," I said, purposely overshooting the year.

"You wish," she said, laughing. "But you're not that far off. I used to be fat, after I had Jeanette. But one day I got serious about my body and I never looked back. I have 1.5 percent body fat."

"I'd challenge you but I left my calipers at the office."

"Don't be a smart ass," she teased. "I can tell you're just trying to play it cool."

"Fine," I said, "take that dress off so I can see what a 1.5-percent-body-fat body actually looks like."

She seemed to know that request was coming because before I could finish, the dress was crumpled on the floor in an electric green ball. She wore matching bra and panties of sheer, black fabric. There were no discernible tan lines on any part of her body. Every scrap of skin was shaded a warm chestnut, like an antique sideboard. In the irregular light of the room, shadows got hung up in the curves of muscle on her arms and stomach and accentuated them beyond their already pronounced state. In the half-light, she resembled an Olympic swimmer on the men's 4 x 100 relay.

"Put your dress back on before Hector sees you."

"Is he here?" she shrieked, looking around.

"He's sitting out front in his car," I told her and motioned to the picture window.

Meredith scurried over to the side of the window and peered around the frame. She tugged at the curtain with both hands as she studied the black sedan.

"You better go easy," I said, "the other drapes are getting jealous." She didn't seem to hear me and wrung the fabric tightly into a coiled-up piece of rope. "Is this an act or does this guy actually make you nervous?"

"How much do you know about him?" she asked.

"I know about the murder in 1963," I answered and successfully spoiled whatever surprise she had in store for me.

"You heard about that?"

"Yes," I replied, "and will you please put your clothes back on? It doesn't seem like you have any intention of sleeping with me, and if that's the case I'd rather not have to study the goods I know I can't afford."

I had no intention of trying to get this transaction transferred to the bedroom, but Meredith seemed like the kind of woman who needed to know she was wanted. She let out a good, honest laugh and gathered her dress up.

"I thought about staying the night," she said as she zipped up the dress, "but I didn't think you'd have the stamina." In a strange way it didn't sound like she was trying to be hurtful.

"Sit down and tell me why you're here," I instructed.

"Is he going to come in?" she asked, staring out the window once more.

"Not unless he breaks in, which, after what's happened today, I don't see as all that remote a possibility. Now will you answer the question?"

"What was it?" she pretended to forget. I let silence help jog her memory. "It really is hot in here," she said.

"Come on, lady—"

"I want you to help find my daughter," she blurted out.

"That's it? You came all the way here to ask me that?"

"Yes," she said, "will you help?"

"Of course I'll help. I'm already working on it."

"But I need you to work for me."

"Does it matter whom I work for as long as Jeanette gets home safely?"

"Yes, it does."

Meredith rambled incoherently as she explained the difference. None of it made any sense but there was something beneath the surface that was being left unsaid and her words walked delicately around it.

"Forgive me if this is too forward," I interrupted, "but when I first spoke to you regarding your daughter, you didn't seem to give a damn. What's changed?"

"She needs our help."

"Of course she needs our help. She's been away from home for over a week."

"No, I think she's in trouble."

"Lady—"

"She texted me."

That got my attention.

"When?"

"This morning."

"What did she say?"

Meredith pulled it up on her phone and handed it to me. It read, *Tell papa to leave me alone.*

"Who's papa?"

"My father. Your employer," she added.

I went into the contacts folder and pulled up the phone number attached to the text. Then I checked it against the one given me by Valenti.

"What are you doing?" Meredith asked.

"Nothing," I said as I riffled through the folder of documents.

"It's her number," she said icily.

She was right. The numbers matched.

"You didn't have to check," she said, looking hurt as she took her phone back and shoved it in her bag.

"I just wanted to be sure." I gave her a moment to get over it. "What do you think she means by the text?"

"I don't know."

"Are there any problems between your father and Jeanette?"

"She is the golden child," she said with a tinge of animosity.

"I know about the will," I told her. "Jeanette is the sole beneficiary. Jeanette and that museum, of course." She seemed impressed at the level of information I had gathered in such a short time. "Did they have a falling out?"

"I think so."

"What does that mean?"

Meredith explained how, on the day Jeanette disappeared, she first went over to her grandfather's home. She was gone for a short time and when she got back she appeared very upset but didn't want to talk about it. She locked herself in her room. When Meredith went to check on her several hours later, the room was empty.

"Why didn't you tell me this when we first spoke?"

"I don't know."

"What aren't you telling me now?"

"Nothing," she cried. "I just need you to help me get her home."

"Fine, let's go to the police and tell them what's going on. We can use the local news to get the word out." I grabbed the photo of Valenti and Jeanette. "We take this photo and plaster it on the ten o'clock news. Someone is bound to call in a tip."

"No, that wouldn't be appropriate. Dad wouldn't allow it."

"She's *your* daughter, Mrs. Schwartzman."

"You won't understand. And please don't refer to me by that name. I went back to my maiden name after the divorce."

"Where does your ex-husband stand in all this?"

"Wherever he needs to stand to hold onto that silly job," she replied.

"Funny, but I can't see you two together."

"Dad hated him," she responded to the question implied by my comment. "That alone was a good enough reason to marry him."

"What about this fellow with the goatee?"

"Sami?" She blushed. "Did you guys meet?"

"We had a long conversation. About what, I can't be sure."

"That's Sami. Sami Halilayen. He's actually very brilliant, you know."

"Did Jeanette experience any of this brilliance?"

"He's there for anyone who needs it. I'm helping him open a spiritual center out in Reseda where clients can come and practice in a nurturing environment while seeking artistic self-fulfillment."

I began to understand and sympathize with the old man's suspicion that his daughter was blowing through his fortune. Sami was probably one of many parasites latching onto the socialite and riding on her currency coattails to carve out lucrative life endeavors.

Money, as it often is, was starting to feel like the root of the whole thing. Cut off from the main pipeline, Meredith now saw an opportunity to get tapped in again. Her warm feelings and interest in her daughter coincided with the text she received asking Valenti to ease off. Where there was friction there was opportunity.

"Were you and your father ever close?" I asked bluntly. She seemed like the kind of person who needed blunt questions. She answered this one honestly.

"Once. It was a long time ago. And it was very short-lived."

I left it at that. There was a deep sadness in the way she said it, despite her attempt to matter-of-factly brush it off.

"What about enemies?"

"Me?"

"Or your dad."

"It'd be quicker to count his friends," she smiled. "Good old Dad never realized that making so many enemies would eventually come back to haunt him."

Before I could explore what exactly she meant by that comment, Meredith's phone buzzed and she instinctively picked it up. I saw her read through a text and a wry smile cross her lips.

"Jeanette?" I asked.

She shook her head and stared at whatever message came in. Her eyes brightened in the glow cast off by the phone.

"Dad is going to flip when he sees this," she said with a laugh. She rose and headed for the front door. Whatever it said, the text was important enough that she didn't need to talk with me anymore about working for her.

"You're going out the front door?" I reminded her.

In her haste, she had forgotten about Hector sitting in the car outside.

"Of course I am," she said while standing in the foyer. "He doesn't control what I do." She quickly turned around and slipped through the back slider, just like she had when she had originally come in.

☼   ☼   ☼

I slept in on Saturday, which for a corporate guy meant seven-thirty. I brewed up a strong pot of coffee and enjoyed the cool morning air coming through the kitchen window. One thing about Los Angeles is that despite some excruciatingly hot days, the nights and mornings are always pleasant. It was overcast, a staple of Southern California summers, and the gray sky hung heavy above. I took my first cup of coffee to the living room and gazed out the front window.

The car was still there. The black roof and hood glistened with morning dew. I could see the outline of Hector's frame through the passenger window. Sometime in the night he had rolled up the driver's window, probably from the cold. He shifted in the seat in a futile attempt to discover that one position that didn't cause his body to ache. It had to have been a very uncomfortable night's sleep.

I grabbed the coffee, settled in a chair by the window, and with my slippered feet propped up on the sill, I watched the car from the comfort of my house over three very hot, very satisfying cups of coffee.

After a leisurely shower, a little bit of time online to pay some bills, one load of whites, and a quick cleanup of the house, I went outside and sat in the backseat of the sedan.

"Okay, let's talk," I said and offered him a hot cup of coffee.

Hector stretched his stiff body awake and rubbed both his eyes with fat knuckles. He took my coffee but didn't turn around to face me. After a night in the car he looked ten years older than his already advanced age.

"We both have jobs to do," I stated. "We can continue to do this silly little dance that isn't going to accomplish much of anything, or we can find a way to work together and save each of us a whole lot of grief. You need to keep tabs on me and report back to your boss. I get it. And I need to do my thing and not feel like a goddamned five-year-old with a helicopter parent. So here's what I propose. You come with me on every meeting. If you want to drive me, so be it. But when I ask you to do something—whatever it is—you do it. If I want you to wait outside, you wait outside. If I need to see someone on my own, you respect that. In return, I promise to keep no secrets from you. And I am going to start this morning. I know about the incident you were involved in back in 1963. I know it was a relative of Gao Li's and that Valenti might have saved you from doing time. Right now I don't see any connection to what is going on today so I'm fine leaving that alone."

There was no reaction. Hector stared into the cup held tightly in his hands. It looked like he was trying to extract every last bit of comfort he could from the warm coffee.

"Do you accept my offer?" I asked.

Hector finished off the coffee in one long, satisfying gulp and handed me the empty cup.

"Okay," he said.

THE TOURIST TRADE

We met at an organic, single-sourced coffee shop in Silver Lake where they individually brewed you a cup after an interminable discourse on the genealogy of the family who grew the beans we were about to consume. I wasn't in the mood and cut the barista off mid-speech and ordered the house blend. The guy then went into shock as he watched Hector stir enough sugar into his cup to achieve the viscosity of strawberry preserves.

"You should really try it first," lamented the young man behind the counter. "It's not at all as bitter as the coffee you make at home."

Hector acknowledged the comment by topping his cup up to the brim with half-and-half. We then joined Sami at a small table on the patio.

"Greetings," the perpetually happy man said as he beckoned us to sit down. "I cherish the opportunity to spend time with both of you."

"The feeling's mutual," I told him.

The invitation to meet wasn't entirely on the level, so

I needed to play along for a while. I had told Sami that I was interested in sitting down and talking over some "heavy issues" but what I really wanted to learn was any inside information he had on Meredith and Jeanette.

Sami eagerly took the bait and suggested we meet at the coffee shop. He sat Indian-style on an already uncomfortable aluminum chair. That, paired with a gingham shirt and flip-flops, presented a very spiritual image. True to form, Sami spent most of the time talking about himself rather than trying to understand whatever "issue" was ailing me. He explained his personal "journey" through a rhetorical framework for which he was both the interviewer and interviewee. Each question he posed to himself was asked in such a manner that it could elicit only an affirmative response.

"Was I finally ready to greet each day with a sense of purpose?" he asked, replaying the internal dialogue he had some years ago. "Yes, I was. Did I want the happiness that had so far eluded me? Yes, I did."

The third time he asked one of those types of questions, this one about it being the time to discover the secret to achieving a fulfilled life, I burst in and answered for him:

"Yes, it was!" I shouted.

Sami smiled knowingly at my enlightenment on his enlightenment. "And so that was how I found my higher purpose," he announced proudly.

"And what exactly is that purpose?" I asked.

"I uncover one's artistic potential," he explained.

"Interesting," I said because I could think of nothing else to say. In the corporate world, that word was code for "Your work has absolutely no merit."

Sami described with enthusiasm how within every being there is a pool of artistic potential. And that just like the earth's own springs there are some rare instances when the water naturally bubbles up to the surface. But for the vast majority of us, that pool lies untapped, often deep down inside. We spend a lifetime never realizing the artist in all of us.

It was the familiar patter of the self-help guru—the concept that potential is always there; it's just our own unintended actions that are keeping it from being released. That kind of claptrap nonsense soothes many an unsatisfied mind. Better it was to be told that you had the talent but that you were holding it back from its true potential rather than accept the cold reality that we are all marginally talented in some fashion and that few have the will to actually do something with it.

None of it resonated with me but it most certainly would have with someone else.

"Was Jeanette one of your clients?" I asked.

"She is," he corrected in the present tense.

"Have you heard from her?" I probed. "Her mom said something about her running off?"

Sami uncrossed his legs and shifted in his seat.

"I really shouldn't discuss a family matter," he told me but then made a very subtle glance in Hector's direction.

I gave it a moment before reminding Hector that the parking meter needed filling outside.

"We got time," he said.

"I think you should fill it," I repeated.

He knew what I was asking for but that didn't mean he liked it.

"Remember our deal," I reminded him.

Hector shot Sami a cold look before reluctantly getting up and leaving us so we could talk privately.

"There's a lot of negative energy in the house," Sami started without any prodding. "It's not good."

"Over what exactly?"

"An article that came out last night."

"What kind of article?"

"It was in one of the online gossip magazines," he explained. I gave Sami space to elaborate. "Those things are just filled with hate."

"Yeah, I don't much care for them either," I commiserated. "What was the article about?"

He gave it time for the drama to ramp up: "Jeanette," he stated and then his voice drifted into a whisper, "and the baby."

"Baby?" I repeated as my mind processed the new development. I recalled the text Meredith got at my house the previous evening and assumed it was somehow connected to the article being released. Her response last night was even more curious now that I knew the contents of the text. She seemed almost happy that it was published.

"Did you know she was pregnant?"

Sami looked at the table and his silence told me he had known.

"Everyone knew," he explained. There was shame in his voice.

☺   ☺   ☺

I sat in the back of Hector's sedan and read the gossip blog entry on my phone. It was a short blurb about one "naughty little girl" of a "gazillionaire" getting herself knocked up. There was a reference to the museum fight in case anyone didn't pick up which gazillionaire it was referring to. It had the typical snarky sign-off that must have sent Valenti over the edge with rage.

I glanced at the back of Hector's head. If, as Sami had said, everyone knew about Jeanette's pregnancy, then that meant Hector knew but withheld it from me despite our recent agreement. I wanted to confront him immediately except I needed him at that moment. The latest development had given me an idea that the once-random Victorian home in Alhambra wasn't so random anymore.

As we approached the house, I handed Hector a security badge from a former associate who'd been terminated for stealing milk from the communal fridge. Policy for a termination was to escort the fired associate to the elevator and to take their badge so they couldn't get back onto the floor. The associate was a middle-aged white woman from Burbank, but I made Hector put it on anyway, even though he didn't look anything like her.

"If you act like you know what you're doing, people will believe it," I instructed him as I pounded on the metal gate. "People fall for badges all the time."

The same impassive face answered the door. This time I simply grabbed hold of the badge attached to my belt and zip-lined it in front of her face, so close that she couldn't read the words. She leaned back to get a better look but by that time I had muscled past her and stepped into the foyer. Behind me, I heard the zip line of Hector's badge being presented, and he cleverly added "Health Inspectors" to the ruse and followed me into the home.

The once-grand parlor was grand no more. It had been carved up into three or four units separated by makeshift walls and curtains suspended from the ceiling. The room smelled of sour milk and disinfectant. Murmuring and laughter and the faint cries of hungry babies reverberated through the old walls.

My white skin, navy sportcoat, and blue plastic badge convinced the occupants, at least for the moment, that I was some official from the city of Alhambra. Hector in his black ensemble was better suited as a representative from the coroner's office but for now it was enough to cause confusion and some doubt. We took that opportunity to search the premises for Jeanette.

As we cruised through the rooms, I pointed to random things like exposed wiring and dirty medical devices and sometimes to just blank spots on the floor.

"Insufficient firewall," I called out. "Improper wiring. Occupancy clustering." With each mention, Hector scribbled them down on the blank forms we used to screen new job candidates. A black portfolio holding the sheets of paper helped sell it.

"PL5501?" Hector called back.

"5502," I corrected.

We worked our way through the endless maze of "hospital" beds but didn't see Jeanette. All of the occupants were of Asian descent and no one seemed to speak any English. Most of the beds were surrounded by family and flowers and foil balloons and had that infectious joy of being around a new life. In the final room on the ground floor we found a family surrounding a young woman, a girl really, but in this cubbyhole there was no joy, just hushed tones and the specter of the empty crib nearby.

Hector and I worked our way up to the second floor. At the top of the landing glared the woman from the entrance and two orderlies stood behind her. I tried the badge one more time but it had lost its effect and the ensemble didn't budge. So I budged by them. As hands grabbed at me and my coat, I gave up the pretense of the city official and just started shouting for Jeanette. I heard the struggling voice of Hector doing the same. I caught a glimpse as he took one of the orderlies and launched the bulky frame down the hall. The old man still had some get-up in him.

All it took was one person to doubt us and suddenly everyone came to their rescue. People in hospital scrubs poured out of rooms and I felt like I was going to be ripped to shreds by all the hands grabbing at my coat and face.

"Jeanette!" I shouted, pulling at the arms that tried to hold me back from moving toward the last set of rooms.

"Jeanette!" I heard Hector yelling at the other end of the hall.

I fought my way forward as they ripped the coat off my back. That bought me a couple of extra feet as they stumbled and were forced to regain hold of me. I took a swing at someone and that bought me a few more feet. But it was short-lived as the circle closed around me. I put my head down and bullied forward, and as I passed each room, I angled my body to see the occupants inside. It was more of the same, but I had to make sure. At last I came to the final room. By then it felt like the entire complex was riding on my back. My knees gave out and I crumbled to the floor and everyone else crumpled on top of me. Through the melee of arms and legs, I peeked into the last room and saw a familiar face—the rotund Filipina who worked as an aide at the convalescent home where Valenti's ex-wife lived.

We locked eyes for a brief moment, but it was long enough for the surprise to register in her dull eyes. I held her gaze as long as I could, conveying whatever kind of warning I could before I was dragged away.

Hector and I were summarily deposited onto the concrete front yard. My coat and badge were lost. Hector's suit was intact but his Brylcreem hair was in a chaotic state and indicated he'd had a tough go of it, as gale-force winds couldn't disturb that coif. We scrambled to our feet and back to the black sedan down the street. We leaned against the hood, took in each other's condition, and let out a belly-emptying laugh. Not because there was anything particularly funny about what we just went through, but because for the first time it just felt like we were getting closer to bringing the girl home.

Hector's pleasure faded quickly. He took on a sullen expression and looked like he wanted to tell me something.

"You all right?" I prodded.

"I didn't tell you this before," he started, "but maybe I should have. It's about Jeanette."

Hector recalled the day that Jeanette went missing. She had taken a car service to the Valenti compound and was inside with the man himself for quite a while. Hector was replacing a taillight when she appeared at his side and asked if he could drive her home.

"She was crying," he told me.

"Did she say why?"

"I didn't ask. I just drove her back to her mom's."

When they pulled up, she didn't immediately get out of the car. She lingered in the backseat like she wanted to say something and after some time asked him if he had kids.

"I told her I did—one girl and one boy. Three grandchildren, too. She then asked me if I was a good father. I said I didn't know. That maybe she should ask my kids."

Hector apologized for not telling me this earlier, but in his act of contrition, while sincere, it wasn't exactly clear to me what he was apologizing for.

"I never told you she was pregnant," he said.

"You knew she was pregnant just from that one exchange in the car?" I asked incredulously.

"You don't have kids, do you?" he threw back.

"No."

Hector said nothing more, as if that was enough proof. Behind it was the implication that I shouldn't question someone in a club of which I wasn't a member. And this member of the club was coming to an unsatisfactory conclusion about Jeanette's foray into motherhood.

"You don't think she had her baby in there?" he asked, hoping I would tell him that she didn't.

"I don't know," I answered.

We hung around for a little while to see if we could spy the Filipina nurse coming out of the building, but she never showed. There were too many orderlies who knew our faces, and we decided not to risk it any further and leave the area. I made a move to get into the backseat.

"Sit in front," he instructed.

A WOMAN'S SCREAM

We continued east to Arcadia where the owner of the Victorian property had its office. My old real estate agent was growing tired of tracking down information for me on houses that I never intended to buy, but she couldn't risk telling me so on the off chance I was legitimately interested in playing the market.

Hector and I found the building, which was more a storefront than an actual office. On its left was a brilliantly lit dumpling house doing a brisk business before lunch had even started. From the looks of the clientele and cars in the lot, it catered to scores of young Asians capping off a night of cruising and clubs with steaming baskets of pork *shui mai*. On its right was an old lady's brassiere shop that hadn't changed the display window in thirty years and was the heroic stalwart from an era and community that wasn't coming back.

We pulled into an open slot and studied the storefront. The door and windows were heavily tinted and obscured whatever "business" lay beyond it. We went up to the front entrance but the door was locked and our knocks went unanswered. I cupped my hands over the glass to try to see beyond the tint but got nothing but black. I stepped back and noticed faces in the reflection of the glass. I turned to see a group of young Asian men surrounding us. In the middle of the circle was Gao Li.

Gao's initial reaction surprised me. He was more afraid than angry and he glanced around the parking lot like he expected there to be more people coming.

"Where's the cavalry?" he asked, but I didn't understand the reference. When he realized there was none, he got his legs under him and returned to his old self. "You're blocking my door, asshole."

Gao brushed by me and unlocked the front entrance.

"We wanted to talk to you about an old building in Alhambra. It's filled with a bunch of Chinese women and babies. But I don't remember seeing any sign about it being a hospital."

My words spooked a few of his cronies and they peeled off. Even Gao looked a little unsure but he masked it well.

"What does that have to do with me?"

"The owner of the building is a corporation that lists this address," I said and pointed to the building behind him.

"Thanks for letting me know," he said and took a step inside.

"How much do you charge?" I called after him. "I'm sure it's not cheap." One aspect of Gao's New China narrative, one he conveniently left out, was that despite the economic boom vaulting many Chinese into the upper levels of wealth, it didn't mean they actually wanted to raise their families there.

"What do they come over on, tourist visas?" I pressed. "Spend a few weeks in that dump, deliver their babies and leave with US citizenship for their kids. Not a bad deal, depending on the price."

"Take off before you regret it," Gao responded coldly.

Hector didn't like his tone and took a step forward. I reached out and grabbed hold of his arm.

"Hold up, Hector. It's not worth it."

Gao cocked his head.

"What'd you say?" he asked but he directed it at Hector, not me. Gao seemed to be doing a calculation in his head and when he finally came to his answer he took a bold step forward. "Hector Hermosillo?" he asked. "Hector Hermosillo?" he repeated.

I didn't like what was going on at that moment and instinctively pulled Hector toward me. Gao and his cronies started to form a circle around us. I used a car pulling into the lot as a way to put some distance between us and kept pushing Hector in the back, guiding him toward the car. My phone buzzed in my pocket.

"What do you think you're doing?" Jeanette's father shouted before I could even get off a hello.

"What do you mean?"

"Why are you harassing Mr. Li?"

I looked around the parking lot expecting to see Jeff watching us watching Gao. I didn't find him.

"I'm not following. We're here in Arcadia outside his office."

"What?!" he screamed. "You're where?"

"In Arcadia."

"Get out of there before you ruin it entirely!"

"Ruin what?" I asked.

"Just get out!"

Not that I needed any encouragement to leave the area, but his tone grated on me. And I didn't appreciate how he felt the need to boss me around.

"Calm down," I told him. "We'll come to your office."

☺　　　☺　　　☺

The foundation's main entry was unlocked. We found Jeff in his office poring over a folder of papers. There was a new installation behind him. It was the extreme close-up of a woman's face projected onto a ten-by-ten screen. Although she remained very still there were slight movements, a twitch here and there to clue you in that it wasn't a still photograph but an actual video. After about a minute I caught her first blink. She looked Nordic, had cold, dull eyes, and stared impassively at the void before her. After the last installation this work must have been a welcome respite.

"Nice piece," I commented, but Jeff was in no mood to talk art.

"Are you fucking with me?" he shouted.

"Take it easy."

"What did I ever do to you?" It wasn't necessarily a rhetorical question but it was still one of those you didn't need to, or want to, answer. "Seriously," he persisted, "what did I ever do to you?"

"Mr. Schwartzman—"

"Don't 'mister' me, all right? Pretending to be all businesslike after you've fucked me over. I welcomed you into this office. I told you things and was very forthright about everything. And you sat there and listened and then went and stabbed me in the back. I thought we were cut from the same cloth. And now you're pulling out the formalities."

"We're all cut from the same cloth," I told him.

"This isn't a joke."

"It wasn't meant to be a joke."

"Why is he here?" he questioned with an outstretched finger pointed in Hector's direction. Before he would allow me to explain, Jeff commanded that Hector leave the room.

"Let's just relax and talk like adults," I said.

"You ruined the museum for me," he started on another tangent.

"I didn't ruin anything," I countered.

Jeff was a one-punch fighter. He took his shot and if it didn't land, he either ran or moved on to find a heavier weapon. His armory was running thin because he was already reverting to the pity club.

"Gao doesn't want anything to do with me," he moaned. "He called me and said we're through. That he won't support the ballot initiative. He thinks it's a trick. He thinks I am in on it with the old man." I thought about how the direction of this great city could so easily be altered by a cryptically worded ballot initiative started by one unstable man and promoted by an equally, yet differently unstable, man. "How crazy is this world?" he asked as if he could hear my thoughts, but he was referencing something else altogether. "The guy I'd rather see dead as my partner in crime," he said with a laugh. I couldn't tell if he had forgotten Hector was in the room or he made that comment on purpose. "What the hell did you say to Gao to get him to think that?"

I recapped my first uncomfortable meeting when Gao thought I was coming to see him with a peace offer from Valenti. "I don't know how he got that idea," I said, watching for Jeff's reaction. There wasn't much, but I was still certain he had helped foment the idea in one of their many discussions. "Today's meeting was a little unexpected. There was a building in Alhambra, an old Victorian with several Chinese occupants."

"They aren't all related, you know," he said.

"I tracked down the corporation on the deed," I continued, "and that led me out to Arcadia to a development company linked to Mr. Li. We happened to be at the office; I questioned him on it and he flew off the handle."

"Well, why wouldn't he? You're harassing him about some stupid building. No wonder he thinks you're trying to undermine him."

"It's not a stupid building, Mr. Schwartzman."

"Knock the mister crap off."

"It's not a stupid building," I repeated. He already had his next snarky comeback ready and was just waiting for me to finish so he could lob it my way. "Its address is linked to your daughter."

He got as far as the first word when my comment hit him and its meaning finally registered. That wiped the smirk right off his face.

"Jeanette," he whispered. It was the look of legitimate remorse. "What do you mean by linked?"

I explained what Hector and I discovered inside the Victorian house. Jeff listened to the details with a look of both shock and confusion. When I finished, he asked,

"But what does that have to do with Jeanette?"

"You knew your daughter was pregnant, right?"

"Pregnant?" he said in a way that made you feel the nausea he was experiencing. The man grabbed at the thinning hair on the sides of his head and let his hands drag down and tug onto both ears. He muttered something to himself, even using the second-person tense to add to the severity of the personal indictment. I couldn't exactly make it out but it sounded like, "You're such an asshole."

Hector and I diverted our eyes. It was difficult to witness a man's humiliation on something so fundamental as raising a child. I turned to Hector to suggest that we leave him alone with his thoughts.

Then, the room erupted with a woman's blood-curdling scream. I had never heard something so primal. I instinctively ducked and covered my head with my arms. Hector leapt to his feet and pulled the knife from his pocket. Jeff didn't move an inch. He sat at the desk and kept his face buried in his hands.

After a moment I realized the source of the scream came from the art installation on the wall. The woman's face in the video was back to that cold stare but you could see her chest heaving as she recovered from having just wrenched her guts out. She was composing herself for the next scream.

"I can't figure out how to shut it off," Jeff mumbled. The broken man was getting closer to the moment when he would accept defeat and all the ignominy that came with it. He had an expression of serene surrender. But my read on Jeff was slightly off, as he apparently had more fight left in him.

"What do you need from me?" he asked, raising his eyes to meet mine. "I have to do something to help bring Jeanette home."

"If you ask her to do something, do you think she will do it?"

"Probably not," he admitted, "but I can try."

"That's all we want," I told him. "We need your help, Jeff. Ask her to come home."

That seemed to warm his spirits some.

"This nonsense has gone on long enough," he stated, rising from his chair. "It's time to bring her home."

I took his offer for a handshake. He was feeling magnanimous enough to extend the offer even to Hector. The old bastard took a moment but he eventually accepted it.

I glanced up at the video behind Jeff. I didn't know how long the intervals were between screams, but just knowing it was coming cast an unnerving pall over the room. I wanted to be long gone before it happened.

Jeff walked us to his office door but no farther.

"I have a few calls to make to my daughter," he announced. It was good to have him back from the edge. He was a noticeably different person. "And who knows," he added cheerfully. "We get this thing cleared up, perhaps the museum deal can still be salvaged. That's not the priority, obviously," he amended, "but it could be one outcome of all this craziness."

Hector and I left him with his calls and his illusions and made our way out of the foundation's office. We got as far as the elevator before the woman's scream came barreling down the empty hall after us. It was still going as the doors closed to whisk us downstairs.

A TIGHT WINDOW

The drive over to Beverlywood took three times longer than it should have. By the time we parked in front of Nelson Portilla's house, the sun had long since vaporized the marine layer and beat down on us with little obstruction.

After the mini-victory with Jeff Schwartzman, I wanted to speak to the kid's grandmother and solicit her help in bringing her boy home—and Jeanette with him. But Hector, with his dark glasses and knife poking out of his pocket, didn't put many people at ease. The last time they met he violated her home and nearly ran her over in the process.

"I need to speak to her alone," I said, "and convince her it's in the boy's best interest to help us." Hector shot me a look like he had no faith in me and my persuasion capabilities. "You have your doubts?"

"We made a deal," he shrugged.

"Yes, we did."

"It's never good to come between an *abuelita* and her boy," he warned as I approached the house. That gave me pause as I recalled the *abuelita's* other "boy" and his heavily armed thug friends.

"Well, it's better than throwing her son in a head-lock," I shouted back with little to no conviction.

After several knocks, the old woman opened the door and recognized me with a broad smile. She graciously shuffled me inside and as I crossed the threshold I shot Hector a look for doubting me.

I had caught the woman in between weekend tele-novelas. She fumbled with the remote to shut off the television, which took quite a while. I scanned the dusty framed photographs on the console. They were your typical school photos of awkwardly smiling boys many years before they became the tattooed, hardened men of today. Nelson's was easy to spot, with his sweeping hair and brooding eyes and look of ineffectual contempt for the world. The chattering of the commercials now silenced, the old woman cleared a spot for me to sit on the couch. Ten minutes of declining offers to eat and drink everything she had in the house soon followed. I finally accepted a glass of water and a greasy *pupusa* to get her to stop.

"That was delicious," I lied, and brought the discussion back to the original purpose of the visit. "I am worried about Nelson."

The mention of the boy's name brought a sun-spotted hand to her faintly beating heart. Whatever pleasure she got from feeding a stranger in her house was cast aside by a deep sadness that washed over her face. She muttered some words that sounded like a lament and then gently kissed her fingers.

"Let me help you bring him home," I offered and

placed my hand on her knee.

"He no come home," she moaned.

"It's okay, I can help."

"He such a good boy. He my baby," she said softly.

"I understand. And believe me, I want to help."

She stood and got the photo down from the shelf and handed it to me. She said something in Spanish and I picked up the word *"principe"* but nothing else. That word had meaning to me. The only other time I heard it was in reference to a less-than-princely figure. I wondered how accurate it was this time. The woman again kissed her fingers and this time pressed them to the boy's forehead in the photo.

From the back of the house came a high-pitched squeal and the sound of thrashing bodies. Hector emerged from the kitchen door. He carried a chubby, red-faced teenager like he was a little baby, except this newborn had fists. Hector plopped Nelson onto the couch vacated by his grandmother. The overstuffed sofa bounced the kid like a car in desperate need of new shocks.

"I caught him coming out the back window," Hector told me. "He could barely fit," he added.

The old woman rushed over to console her boy. She had a few choice words for Hector who quietly took them like he was the child who had spent a lifetime disappointing her. He let her have her say, which was plenty. Apparently the fact that she lied to me and was just stalling to give her boy time to escape didn't factor into the list of things to admonish. I followed Hector's lead and let her get it all out of her system.

"Nelson, we're trying to help you," I said during a

break in the *abuelita's* recriminations. "Can't you see that?"

"Whatever," he pouted, the word every teenager resorted to when they had nothing to say.

Hector made a move toward him, but I held out my arm to intercept.

"Can we talk together in the back?" I asked the boy. I needed to get him away from the security blanket to his left and the menacing figure in front of him. I gestured for him to follow me. He reluctantly took my lead and got up from the couch. Once more I had to tell Hector to stay behind. He shot me a look and then glanced at the old woman, whose eyes bored in on him.

"I'll go outside," he decided. "Lock the windows," he advised as he went out the front door.

Nelson's room was smaller than a junior walk-in closet. Twin beds placed in one of the corners created a perfect L-shaped "couch." I sat first. The bed creaked and sagged so much that I feared I wouldn't be able to stand up without a struggle. Nelson wasn't fully committed and remained in the doorway.

The walls were plastered with a collage of music posters, fashion magazine pages, and his own photographs. The black-and-white photos were of an artistic bent with their Dutch angles and extreme close-ups. There was an inordinate number of reflection shots— through mirrors, glass doors, and off ponds and puddles. I marveled at youth's unceasing ability to seek depth in shallow pools.

I pointed to one of the few photos with human subjects. It was a close-up of Nelson and Jeanette, cheeks pressed together, smiling up at the camera held an arm's length away.

"You two look happy," I said.

Nelson didn't bother to look up. He stared at some random spot on the carpet like he was trying to burn a hole through its already thin threads. A duffel bag packed nearly full of clothes sat on the floor close to the spot where Nelson focused all of his intense attention.

"Where were you going with all of that?" I asked. Failing to get him to engage, I tried a different tack. "Did you learn how to drive a stick shift yet?" I teased. This kid had some anger in him, and if there was any chance of getting him to talk, I was going to have to engage that anger.

"Don't take this the wrong way, Nelson, but you're an idiot. Guys like you and me—but definitely guys like you—" I clarified after giving him the once-over, "don't take on guys like Valenti."

I was intentionally casual about my delivery to try to convey an inevitableness to what I was about to tell him. "Do you know how much money he has? Whatever money you think he has, multiply it by a thousand, and then you'll be halfway there."

"You think I care?"

"You should. That kind of money buys you things, and I don't mean stuff like a home better than this." I made a dismissive gesture to the shabby surroundings.

"That's how we're different," he said, mustering some self-righteousness, "because that kind of thing don't matter to me."

"*Doesn't* matter," I corrected. "And you'd like to think it doesn't, but it does. With his kind of dough people can be bought for a price. Me—why else would

I be wasting my time here with you? That old *pachuco* out front, you—"

He scoffed. I gave it a brief pause.

"Jeanette."

"You don't know her," he shot back.

"I don't have to."

"She doesn't even care about money."

"Rich people always say that."

"She's different," he countered. "You wouldn't even know it when talking to her that she's super rich. She's just a regular girl," then realizing how inadequate that sounded, he appended, "but also different. Special."

All along I never thought that Nelson's involvement with Jeanette's disappearance had any trace of a malicious nature. His strident defense of his girl made me wonder if all of this was simply over the star-crossed young love of two kids from disparate neighborhoods. A for-profit school with a mission for diversity brought them together. A baby eventually came out of it. It seemed so antiquated for contemporary Los Angeles, and for what seemed like a fairly progressive family, but some prejudices run silent and they run very deep.

"Do they not like you?" I asked, keeping the subject of the potential hatred broad. I wanted him to fill it in.

"Who?"

"Her family."

"They don't care enough about her to worry about me," he said.

I felt a dull pang in my chest and subconsciously rubbed my shirt back and forth as if warming it up would make it go away. It was one of those feelings that sometimes reared up on the commuter bus ride home at dusk or in the audience of one of those unnecessary conferences I always had to attend. It was that disquieting feeling of being alone.

I thought of Jeanette, the shelves of self-help books, her distracted parents, her lying in that clinic surrounded by strangers, and I felt for the first time a real need to find her. I didn't necessarily need to bring her home, just find her and talk to her. I'd figure out what I would say later.

"All right, I'm in," I told him.

He looked at me quizzically.

"In on what?" he asked.

"Whatever it is you guys are trying to do. I'll help by getting the old man off your backs."

I could see Nelson internally deliberate the offer. He was trying to determine if this was a trick. Overselling the offer would only increase his suspicion that it was a trap, so I decided to pull back a bit in order to enhance its legitimacy.

"I don't even want to hear the plan. I assume it's a horrible one," I said with disgust. "But I'll do what I can. Probably won't be successful but I will try."

"Why?"

"Why what?"

"Help us."

"You look like you could use it."

After some shuffling of feet and more pouting, I got him to agree on a place and time to meet later that night. I tried to get him to bring us to Jeanette but he wouldn't go for it.

"I have to talk to her first," he explained. "You guys show up with me…she wouldn't forgive me if I did that."

I didn't have much choice but to trust him.

"Okay," I agreed. I proffered my hand and shook the dead fish he offered back. "Come on, kid, first thing you have to do is tighten up that shake."

I left a smiling Nelson to finish packing and walked back to the car where Hector waited by the driver's door. He looked past me as if expecting to see Nelson in tow.

"We're going to meet him tonight at a Rally's out in the Valley," I explained. Off his quizzical look, "He's going to bring Jeanette with him."

Hector said nothing but he didn't have to. I could hear the doubt in his silence.

"He'll bring her," I said.

He didn't bring her. He didn't even bring himself.

We wasted four hours driving out to Sunland and sitting in a Rally's parking lot waiting for Nelson and Jeanette to show. But they never did. Just as we were about to call it a night, Hector's phone buzzed.

"Is it her?" I asked.

"No," he said and studied the number. "It's Valenti."

We both sensed what was about to happen next. I observed Hector answer and casually look away to some random spot across the parking lot as he listened to the old man. It was a short conversation.

"He wants to meet us at the club," he said.

Hector said nothing on the drive. Perhaps it was my imagination, but he started to resemble the Hector I knew when we first started out on this work. He was morphing back into his old role before my eyes. Or, I was projecting my feelings onto him because I knew at the end of this drive I was going to be fired.

I knew the termination walk very well. I had walked it too many times with associates not to recognize that feeling of a distinct distance growing around me. The banter, if there was any, was small talk of a different sort than the kind that took place around the coffee machine or in the elevator. There, you talked of the weather and last night's game to non-sports fans. Here, you made hollow observations on anything at all just so you wouldn't have to listen to the silence.

"Be nice once they open up another lane on the 110 interchange," I said, but Hector never acknowledged me.

I desperately wanted to crawl into the backseat for the remainder of the ride.

DEAD MAN WALKING

We pulled into the loop under the Coverdale Building and parked under the canopied entrance, a completely unnecessary design as the building above already shielded us from rain and sun. Rows of exposed light bulbs lit up the space like a Broadway theater.

Inside, I was led to the antiquated dining room and pointed to a table in the corner where Valenti sat. He was the only person in the room. I assumed members preferred the Malibu chapter of the club on the weekends. The tuxedoed fellow who was helping me eyed my coatless frame and quietly brought over the house's blue blazer with shiny gold buttons. I slipped it on and made the long walk across the burgundy carpet. I slowed as I reached the table and took the coat off. I was growing tired of being told what to do.

Valenti started to dress me down before I even took my seat. I held out my hand to stop him.

"No more speeches," I said. "Not today."

I looked around for the waiter. Valenti wasn't going

to offer me anything and I was damn determined to get a free cocktail out of the deal before being dismissed. I tried to think of one of the expensive, aged scotches but none of the names immediately came to mind so I ordered a gin instead. A double.

"What happened in 1963?" I asked after a long pull on the glass.

"That's not what we are here to discuss."

"Yes, it is. You pushed me in that direction." I gestured to the area by the entrance. "You insisted that I work closely with Hector. You insisted that I talk to Gao—"

"Jimmy," he corrected with his usual smirk.

"What actually happened that day?"

I didn't expect him to answer, and he obliged.

I was coming to the uneasy conclusion that I was being played the entire time. All along it wasn't about his granddaughter; it was about the museum and Gao and getting what he wanted. Jeanette might just have been a pawn in the whole thing.

"Was Hector covering up for you? Or did you cover up for Hector to gain his loyalty? Whatever this feud was between you and Li, I imagine it manifested itself in some sort of proxy war among the people down a few levels. At least you paid Hector back with some lifetime employment driving you around. I guess that was a fair bargain. The other guy didn't fare so well."

Valenti stared at me with no emotion.

"And now it's all come full circle with the younger Li," I said, being deliberately vague with the details. He took the bait.

"How do you mean?"

"Just what I said. He's involved. And maybe trying to exact a little payback."

I decided to leave it at that. If I was going to be dismissed, there was no reason to give him any information I had discovered. Hector would probably fill him in later anyway.

Valenti was intrigued by the developments I alluded to. I wanted to pretend that didn't mean anything to me but it did. In a strange way I felt all along like I needed to impress this man, or the money that elevated this man to such stature. Sometimes we look for validation wherever we can get it.

"Why'd you hire me in the first place? Look, I am my own biggest fan, but if I wanted this task done, and done right, I would have hired a real private investigator or gone to the police."

"Ironically, you were hired for the same reason you're being dismissed—indiscretion."

He slid over a printout from a local gossip blog.

"You know I didn't place that article," I said. "But you're pissed off or scared or humiliated or whatever it is and you're going to relieve yourself as you have all your life—on someone else. So if it makes you feel better, have your speech about indiscretion. At least let me order another drink."

I pointed to my glass, and the attentive waiter hurried off to bring a refresher.

"By the way," I said when the waiter returned. "She had the baby. That's probably what the $45,000 was for— to pay for the right to have her baby in some crummy building in Alhambra with a bunch of strangers."

"What?" he whispered.

"Trust me that you wouldn't want to see this place. Ten to a room, not exactly sanitary. Hector can fill you in," I told him, somewhat uncomfortable with the cruelty of the words coming out of my mouth. "Maybe because she didn't know where else a sixteen-year-old with no support can go to have a baby. Or maybe the family didn't want her to have that baby. You would know why, not me."

"I'll make your life a living hell," he hissed, white spittle forming on his lip.

"Too late," I replied. "Now that I give it some thought, I think you knew about the baby the whole time. At least at the very end before she went 'missing.' You conveniently left out those little details," I reminded. "So before you give me another speech about indiscretion or whatever, look within, pal, look within."

That's when I noticed the check on the table written out to me for 5,000 lousy dollars. I asked the hovering waiter for his pen and full name and then endorsed the check over to him.

"Better cash that now before he cancels payment," I instructed as I handed the man the check.

I went out the front entrance, passed the idling sedan where Hector sat behind the dark glass, and grabbed the first available taxi for the long and expensive trip back to Eagle Rock.

HOG-TIED

Pat Faber set up a six-thirty touch base on Monday morning as a not-so-subtle reminder that he was still in charge. Normally, calling in was accepted for any meeting starting before 8 a.m., but with a touch base you had to do it in person.

Touch-base meetings, at which people just talked to each other, were the darlings of the corporate world. For managers, it was tangible proof that associate feedback was important to them. For associates, it was the opportunity to talk about your accomplishments and hint at the need for a salary increase, something your manager never truly acknowledged and certainly never did anything about.

I always followed a standard approach. I would come with a list of three topics. Never more than three because that would overwhelm Pat, and when that happened he assumed that the person overwhelming him had a communication problem. At the end of my agenda of three I would always drop, "…and one thing I need your advice on." Pat relished the opportunity to pass along wisdom, so I would quickly roll through my three items, always presenting the challenge first and then how I overcame it. We'd then spend the remaining twenty minutes of the thirty-minute touch base going over the issue I needed help on. To be sure, the issue was never a real one and if it was, I already knew the answer. But Pat saw it as something I really struggled with. The value of the touch base was measured by the amount of time Pat talked. Sometimes he'd speak for the entire meeting and when it was time to leave, he was so energized that he'd show me to the door and with a slap on the back he'd say, "We need to do these more often."

That's how I kept off management's radar. But on this particular Monday morning, I flirted with danger. Distracted by my work outside the office, irritated that I had to drag myself into work on a Monday just as the sun was creeping over the horizon, pissed off that they had yet to replace the half-and-half in the break room, I walked into Pat's office without an agenda.

"Whatcha got for me, Chuck?" Pat chirped a level or two louder than was needed in the empty offices.

"What a week," I stumbled. "I'm barely keeping my head above water."

Pat nodded but he didn't like it. "Busy" was an acceptable reply in elevator banter but not in a touch base.

"Well, that's why they pay us," he reminded me.

We bandied about a couple of things I was working on but we never quite got into a good rhythm. I was distracted and my words showed it. Pat grew frustrated and decided to take the lead.

"What do you think of this whole obesity thing?" he asked casually. I was taken aback. All along I never felt my co-manager Paul's relentless focus on eradicating obesity from the firm ever garnered much support, but here was Pat taking up the mantle. He either believed in the cause or it was just a ploy to stir the pot holding the two people about to duke it out for head of the group. "The health costs are becoming prohibitive," he added. "We really need to help these poor people."

Now I was nervous. Pat was quoting verbatim from Paul's messaging plan. When you can get someone to repeat what you say, you have won the game. I knew not to dismiss Paul's idea outright—that would not be received well, even if the receiver was not a fan of it. I had to tread carefully.

"It's a real concern," I started solemnly. "It's something that's going to take the full attention and resources of our group."

I foolishly hoped that would be enough. It wasn't.

"So what would you do?" he asked straight out.

"There's no silver bullet solution," I began tentatively, "but more a series of smaller efforts and initiatives." I babbled on like this for a minute-plus, which must have felt like twenty. It was all empty jargon, and Pat wasn't buying a word of it. "Anyway, it's something I'd need to get my head around and put out a recommendation, or something."

I had flown under the radar in enemy territory for a long time but it felt like I was about to be discovered. My reputation was built on being an innovator but the truth was I hadn't had a fresh idea in over ten years, and even that idea wasn't very original. The Stoplight System was a "revolutionary" program aimed at curbing sexual harassment in the office. All I really did was repackage work already in existence into an easier-to-understand format. As long as I played along and talked a good game, no one seemed to notice or care that I hadn't done anything meaningful since then The real concern wasn't that I had no ideas; it was that management would figure it all out. But reputations, once built, are very hard to undo. Thankfully, no one ever looked that closely.

"Chuck, you haven't had a fresh idea in ten years."

My heart skipped.

"If you're going to take this group to the place it needs to be, you're going to have to bring a new perspective, a new vision." The lecture that ensued was as direct a dressing-down as the corporate world ever saw. They were very rare, and that did not bode well for me.

"You're right," I mustered like an already defeated man.

There was a long, uncomfortable pause.

"Nothing for me?" he asked like the seventh kid after a six-pack of sodas has been passed out.

"No," I answered, though I wished I did have something. "Not this week."

"Thank you, Chuck." He dismissed me without getting up.

I scurried out of his office before anything more was said and nearly ran over Paul on his way in.

"Hey, Chuck," he smiled. "Little touch base with the boss?"

"Yeah, we just wrapped up."

"Did you touch them all?" He laughed at the same joke he'd been telling for fifteen years.

"Yes, Paul, I touched them all."

"Hey Chuck," came the earnest voice, "I've been meaning to talk to you about all this…craziness. I just want to say ahead of time that there are no hard feelings." Why would there be any, I thought to myself. "No matter how this turns out, whether it's you running the group or me, I'm going to be happy. Because at the end of the day, it's the group that matters, and with you or me at the helm it's going to be a huge success."

It was a terrific speech, and I didn't believe a word of it.

"Paul, thank you for those kind words. You have to know that I feel the same way about you. And if put to a choice," I said, placing a hand on his shoulder and mustering up a level of unctuousness to match his, "I think you are the better man for the job."

"I believe you, Chuck, when you say it." The bastard somehow got a tear in his eye. I could compete with Paul on many things, but false sincerity was not one of them. If he went in for a hug I might have punched him.

"There are my boys," Pat said, smiling and watching over the proceedings from his office door like a spectator with a fistful of crumpled bills. "Sizing up the competition, are you?"

Paul and I played it off like good sportsmen do, but I resented the cockfight element of it and the way Pat stood over us with that glib smile at his "boys" who were about to be pitted against each other in a fight for their corporate lives.

Pat never had to fight for anything and was kept around for fear of an ageism lawsuit. And still he clung on despite the firm stripping him of any kind of responsibility. I hated that old man because he was a dithering fool who believed he was gifted. I hated him because he made it and men like my old boss, Bob Gershon, didn't. I hated him because this was the man who controlled my destiny. And it was at that very moment that I decided I actually wanted the job.

I didn't want the responsibility of the role, or the bump in salary, or the juicy title that came with it. I didn't want the A-level parking spot or the secret double-bonus opportunities that opened up once you entered this rarified layer of upper management. I wanted it because I wanted to shove it down Pat Faber's throat.

"Make sure you touch 'em all," I advised Paul and stormed off.

☺   ☺   ☺

Despite any misgivings I had of ever using Badger for any work assignments, I needed him for some personal use because, even though Valenti had fired me from the job, I was nowhere near ready to quit. For some reason I simply felt like I owed it to Jeanette to find her and make sure she was safe.

I had placed a call to Badger the night I was dismissed by Valenti with a request to track down the real name and address of the gossip blogger who wrote the story about Jeanette. These sorts of mentions were universally placed by sources with motives—mostly public relations hacks but also people with personal axes to grind. Perhaps there was value in knowing what motivation drove the person who placed this particular story. Badger told me he would have the information to me in a few hours. But I never heard back from him.

After several attempts to reach him and having his phone go straight to voicemail, I decided to make the short drive over to his office/home in Echo Park during the lunch hour. In my previous dealings with him, the one constant was his reliability. Like many of his self-proclaimed merits, his "Johnny-on-the-Spot" moniker was consistently accurate. My mind raced at the possibilities and the growing fear that I, and my amateurish sleuthing, had set him on a course that had brought him into harm's way.

I looked apprehensively at the large bay windows outside his office but couldn't see past my own noonday reflection in the glass. I crossed the ten feet of sidewalk to the front door and entered the office.

It was ten degrees hotter inside than out. The air was still and rank. I didn't see Badger, but the half-opened curtain leading to the back room sang out that if I wanted my answer, I needed to cross through it. My feet sank in the gold-plush carpet as I moved toward the back of the room. Passing the desk, I lifted up the yellowed newspaper. The gun was not there.

The curtain dividing the office space from the living quarters hung heavy on a metal rod. As I pushed it aside I took a step forward and leaned back at the same time; the bottom half of my body entered the room while my head remained in the doorway. I knew what was back there but wasn't quite ready to confront it.

I saw the awkward figure sitting on the floor with its back to the wall. He was shirtless and had his hands bound behind him. His head, covered in a pillowcase, slumped down onto his shoulder in an unnatural position.

I suddenly felt nauseous and fought off a bout of the dry heaves. Then I heard rustling and realized that Badger was moving.

"Jesus!" I shouted and ran over to him. I ripped the pillowcase from his head and his hairpiece came with it. Even with the labored breaths reverberating throughout the room, it still felt like I was looking at a dead man. His skin was a sickly white, his eyes bloodshot.

"There he is," his voice scratched, lacking its normal enthusiasm. "Give me a little water, would you?"

I found a never-washed glass on the sink in the bathroom and filled it up. I held it to his lips and he greedily drank from it. Most of the water just rolled down his chest, but those few swallows put some of the life back into him.

"What happened?" I asked.

He muscled himself upright. I heard the grinding of metal on metal as the handcuffs that bound his wrists rubbed against the drainpipe they were looped around. The skin under the cuffs was raw and even bloody, and blood spots on the pipe glistened against the rust, showing he had struggled mightily to break free.

"Get the key," he instructed. "It's in the top right drawer of the desk."

I scrambled back to the front room and found the key among a pile of metal paperclips and bent thumb tacks. I thought of the humiliation he must be feeling, the equivalent of a cop having his squad car stolen. Badger had been overcome and bound with his own handcuffs.

It took me a few tries but I was finally able to release his wrists. "You're a prince," he whispered and went into the bathroom to splash cold water on his face.

"Tell me what happened," I said as he returned to the room, recovered his hairpiece, and put it back on its rightful spot.

"It's nothing," he said.

I detected a tinge of embarrassment.

"What do you mean it's nothing? Who did this? Did you get a look at them?"

"Don't worry about it."

"I'm very worried."

"It's not that," he dismissed. "It's just something we do."

"Wait…what? Something *who* does?"

"Yeah, a little role-play me and my lady friend like to do." He might as well have said something about taking out the trash. It was a non-event in his eyes. "I must have said something that upset her. I never thought she'd take this long to get back." He turned to face me. "Guy, I let you down."

The man responsible for unearthing the seamy side of potential employment candidates, the one whom I was about to rely on to help me track down Jeanette, was too busy getting himself hog-tied to radiators to complete his duties and was asking for forgiveness. And for some reason I wasn't even angry.

"I found your gossip blogger," he said. "Sorry I couldn't get this to you earlier but I was preoccupied."

He handed me a slip of paper with a name and address. Putting aside whatever misgivings I had about his personal life and overall demeanor, I decided to engage him on a long-term assignment to help me track down Jeanette. He could do things I couldn't and he had already proven to be very handy in unearthing information.

"I have another job for you," I told him. "A big job."

I explained everything to him, including details I'd withheld from Detective Ricohr. Badger nodded solemnly but the obligatory declaration of this job being the top priority never came. Instead, he sort of stalled like there was something more to be said.

"Does that all make sense?"

"Perfect sense," he replied. "Full commitment required."

"I would imagine."

"Job could go in many directions."

"Most definitely," I said.

"And for an indeterminate length."

"I guess so."

He nodded his head but not in agreement.

"And this one isn't for the company?" he asked.

That's when I finally understood his apprehension. The job was sizable, and I hadn't delivered on my half of the deal.

"What kind of retainer do you usually work on?" I asked. I had seen enough of the old movies to know how this worked.

"Let's not make this about money, guy," Badger scolded. "I'm helping you because you're a stand-up guy who has always done right with me. I don't work with just anyone, you know. This can be an ugly business and I am careful with whom I associate."

It was all an act—the man clearly needed cash. I could see the army cot and hotplate and empty cans of refried beans and squeaky fan doing nothing against the heat. But there was the man's pride to deal with. He needed to be begged.

"I insist. This is a big job."

"I know what I am getting into."

"And I can't allow you to put forth such a big effort without an equal commitment on my end."

"I know you're good for it." He waved me off but quickly added, "But if you insist, my standard fee is 400 a day plus expenses." I was a little taken aback by how quickly he gave in. Times must have been worse than I thought. I went out to my car and got my checkbook. As I wrote out a check, Badger wet his lips in apparent anticipation of an expensed meal on my dime.

"One week advance good enough?"

"Whatever you think is right is right with me," he kept up the charade. "And don't feel you have to—"

"Take the fucking money, Badger," I said, growing annoyed.

"You're a prince," he smiled as the check disappeared, with some effort, into the narrow slit of his two-sizes-too-small jeans back pocket.

He walked me out, a little lighter on his feet and showing no effect of the $2,800 of my money weighing him down. What started out as a side job to get central air in my house was turning into a gaping hole in my already bleak bank account. But I couldn't begrudge Badger. This was, after all, his livelihood, and who was I to extort him just because I happened to save him from dehydration caused by a temperamental dominatrix.

Out on the sidewalk, he gave me a sweaty hug and declared I was, yet again, his number-one priority.

PROGRESS

I got out of work a little early—like most people in corporate American do every day—and made the drive out to North Hollywood where the blogger lived. Traffic was decent for the 101 and I soon found myself steaming up and over the Cahuenga Pass and down into the Valley.

The San Fernando Valley was a figurative, and on days like today, a literal purgatory. Flat, hot, and endless, the monotony of the basin mirrored the lives of the nameless people living there. The temperature outside flirted with a hundred degrees but never quite committed to triple digits despite its best efforts.

The apartment complex was deep in North Hollywood where the streets and buildings were laid out in perfect symmetry, inheriting the same form and function of the orange groves they replaced decades prior. I went through glass doors that led to an open courtyard where a blue-green pool sat untouched for yet another year. The apartment was on the second floor in the back, and I took one of the four outdoor staircases.

The woman who answered the door was a frumpy maiden much younger than her image let on. She lived in a cramped studio with sagging bookcases and a worn throw rug on top of even more worn wall-to-wall carpet. She led me to a spot before a small air conditioner that was as effective against the heat as a fan blowing air over a bowl of ice cubes. I sat on a cheap folding chair. She relaxed on the edge of a futon and pulled one leg up under the other so she could pick at her toenails while she spoke.

"I got an email through the site and it just said that they had information on a family member of an important man in the city. They were vague with the details, particularly how important this man was." She retold the events leading to the publishing of the article with a detached, almost bored expression. It was as if she wanted to convey to me that this job didn't matter to her and she rather hated it but was resigned to doing it. For now, anyway.

"Then what happened?"

"Nothing. Total radio silence. I wrote it off as a crank—you get a lot of these. Though part of me sensed this one was legit, I wrote back and never got a reply. Until four days ago. I got an email late in the night that laid out all the details, the baby out of wedlock, the underage angle, and most importantly, the identity of the important man."

"Who was it?" I asked. I needed to confirm if we were talking about the same family. The woman eyed me suspiciously, trying to figure out my angle, if there was one.

"If you represent the family, then you should already know, right?"

"But I first need to know if you know."

"Oh, I know who it is."

"Did you verify the source?" I asked.

"Of course I did. I wouldn't have pushed the story otherwise." There was an element of nicked pride in her response, as if she was hurt that I questioned her ethics in publishing unseemly stories about people's private matters.

"And they are credible?"

"As credible as it gets," she responded mysteriously.

"What does that mean?"

She suddenly felt the power shift over to the futon and took the opportunity to exploit it.

"Can we work out a deal?" she asked tentatively. She was as new to the shakedown as I was. I had stopped by the ATM on the way, expecting this moment. I placed twenties in various amounts in various pockets in case she played hardball and I could claim "all the money I got" routine. Little did I know that fifty bucks was all it would take. I gave her the extra ten because I felt bad for her.

"So who was the source?"

"The source was the source," she answered with a riddle and the annoyingly sly expression people make when telling riddles.

"Your source was Jeanette Schwartzman?"

The woman touched the side of her nose. We apparently were switching from riddles to charades.

"How did you know it was her?" I asked, still not quite believing it. The logic wasn't working.

"It was her. We met in person, and she had pictures on her phone with Carl Valenti. She looked just like the girl in the photos. And they knew details that made me very comfortable they were who they said they were."

"Who was she with?"

"Some boy, sort of effeminate, probably Hispanic but I shouldn't guess ethnicity without being sure." I had never believed Nelson was involved in anything nefarious but now it was a question if he and Jeanette were in on something nefarious together. "I don't think he was the father."

"Why do you say that?"

She gave me a "don't make me say it out loud" look. She wasn't comfortable discussing people's ethnicity and it seemed she was equally uncomfortable discussing people's sexuality.

"Let's just say the baby didn't look like him," she said, avoiding anything inappropriate. For a gossip blogger, she held pretty high standards.

The fact that the person behind the placement of the story was the subject of the story itself was a puzzler that I still couldn't quite comprehend. I probed to see if Jeanette gave any kind of insight into why she was doing it.

"I asked her that. She was vague and didn't really want to answer. She was quick to point out that it definitely wasn't for money. I sort of believed her."

I moved off the events in the past and focused my attention on the future. Standard practice in Corporate America was to conclude every meeting with someone asking, "What are our next steps?" It was an admirable attempt to convince everyone that, although we had just sat around talking nonsense for fifty-five minutes, it wasn't without purpose and we needed concrete proof that it was all worthwhile. Humans have an en-during desire to feel like we are making progress.

For me, I didn't want to let a lever go un-pulled. I needed this woman as an ally if Jeanette ever contacted her again. And although it was unlikely, perhaps she could be used to lure the girl back home. But I didn't want the woman to think that she could exploit this situation for more money. Given her recent negotiation skills, I deemed this risk rather low.

"We could use your help, if you are up for it." I handed her my business card and scribbled my personal number on the back. "If you ever hear from Jeanette, please call me first. The family would be grateful."

She watched me take a quick glance around the cramped studio apartment and her face expressed a look of shame. I never intended to make her feel bad. It was an unfortunate habit of mine when meeting people like her in Los Angeles. I felt the urge to piece together their history that led them to their current situation—a bright, personable-enough woman with a set of values still intact, sitting in a crummy apartment, picking her feet, and waiting for the sun to go down to provide at least a modicum of relief from the heat.

"Never thought I'd end up in a job like this," she said, as if sensing what I was wondering.

I pointed to the card she held in her hand.

"If some copy editor positions open, I'll let you know. We could always use a good proofreader."

This appeared to bring a little bit of brightness to her day. My desire for progress equaled everyone else's.

With one step in purgatory, I decided to make the full leap into hell.

Pacoima was another ten miles from the North Hollywood apartment. On the drive there, the flirting-with-triple-digits heat was consummated and never looked back. The change in temperature from the climate-controlled car to the blacktop surface of the parking lot at Sheila Lansing's convalescent home involved a thirty-degree swing. The initial thrust was oddly pleasant, like the first moments of a hot shower. But then the oppressive nature of the heat enveloped me and for a brief instant, I thought I would collapse on the walk from my car to the front door of the home. The heat coming off the pavement somehow felt hotter than the one scorching the back of my neck.

The handle on the glass door was as hot as a pan left carelessly over an unattended burner. I scurried into the lobby and eagerly breathed in the antiseptic-scented air.

"It's a hot one," the front desk attendant chirped.

"My word," I replied. "How do you handle it?"

"It's a dry heat, so it's not so bad." Dry or not, that kind of heat was unbearable.

"I'd like to see Sheila Lansing."

"Why, of course. Let me have someone show you there." She picked up the phone and scanned the numbers. "The old girl is getting quite a treat today," she said absently.

"Why's that?" I asked.

"So many visitors in one day."

The attendant put the phone down when she saw a young man in scrubs passing by. She asked him to escort me upstairs. I looked around and but didn't see the attendant I was really interested in.

"Is the other attendant in?" I asked casually. "I forget her name but she's Filipino, dark hair, wears it in a braid...." They didn't seem to make the connection. "A little heavy-set?"

The front desk attendant and my escort shared an awkward look.

"Tala? She's not here today."

"Do you expect her?"

"Hard to say, honestly."

There was hesitancy in her voice. To me it sounded like Tala hadn't been to work in a while and no one seemed to know why.

I was led upstairs to the second-floor balcony. A mister and fan system blew micro-droplets of water that provided instant relief when it touched your skin but tasted like rust when you breathed it in.

Sheila was in her normal spot, covered again in a blanket though this time with a light cotton fabric. She was the only resident out at that time.

"Ms. Lansing, the heat index is—" but the old woman cut off the attendant before he could finish his warning.

"If I like it, I like it," she reasoned with a dismissive wave. "You're back," she said to me.

"Surprised to see me?"

"A little. Must be bad news," she guessed. "What happened to her?"

"She hasn't come home."

"That's not so bad."

"And she's a new mom." I let those words sink in. She stared at me but didn't give much up. "Why didn't you tell me?"

"If you only recently found out yourself, then that means Carl didn't tell you either. Did you ask him why he kept it a secret?"

"I did."

"Did he give you an answer?"

"Nope."

"But you want one from me. Okay, I will prove I am the better person. I like her and didn't want to betray her confidence."

"When's the last time you spoke to her?"

"It's been a while. Not since before you and I last met."

"Have you tried to contact her?" I asked.

"Now that you tell me she has had the baby, I just might."

"Do you happen to know where she is staying? Even if it's just a town, that'd be helpful."

"I don't."

Clearly she wasn't in the frame of mind to give up much information. I asked her to let me know if she heard from Jeanette. And if she did talk to her, that she try to persuade the girl to return home. The old woman acknowledged the request but didn't say outright whether she was going to agree to it.

"Whatever happened to that nurse, the angry one?"

"She hasn't shown up for work this week. Why do you ask?"

"Just curious."

I leaned back and looked down at the empty rows of glide chairs.

"Not a lot of visitors today," I commented. "Must be the heat."

"There aren't many on any day," said Sheila. "You're my first visitor in a while," she felt the need to add, and instantly gave herself away.

We chatted about nothing for a couple of minutes longer, mostly about the heat, then I got up to excuse myself. A few feet from the door, I turned back.

"Just so you know," I told her, "I'm not working for Carl anymore. He dismissed me over an indiscretion that I didn't commit. He knew I didn't do it but he fired me anyway. If I had to guess, this outcome was inevitable all along and if I was smart I would just go home and mind my own business.

"But I'm not smart and I'm not ready to quit. I've never met this kid; I don't have anything at stake in it, but somehow I still feel responsible for bringing her home. Maybe her family is screwed up but most families are. It's still better than being out there all alone."

I made it no more than three steps toward the door.

"Sit back down, please," she instructed. Once I was back in the chair, she admitted that she had seen Jeanette earlier that morning. I assumed she had but didn't tell her so. "She has a handsome little baby."

"So it's a boy?"

"Yes, Carl has his heir," she spat. "You know that I am childless?"

"You mentioned it before."

"But you don't know why." I told her I didn't. "Let's just say it wasn't because of a lack of desire and it wasn't because of a lack of ability."

"So what other reason is there?"

"Fear," she answered. "Fear of Carl."

"You're going to have to elaborate, Ms. Lansing,

because if I am understanding you correctly that is a pretty big accusation."

"I didn't make an accusation; I just described a feeling I had," she parsed as if in fear of a defamation suit. "I was scared of what he could do. He is, as you may guess, prone to abusive behavior."

"That's still a broad term. What kind of abuse are you referring to?"

"Well, I never had a child," she replied. "That should answer it for you. And that's why I don't think Jeanette should go back to that household."

"But she lives with her mother," I reminded her. "And could even stay with her dad if she wanted to."

She smiled at me.

"I've heard about those two from Jeanette. They will do anything to stay on Carl's good side. There's too much money in it," she said, and despite the ugliness in her words there was a vein of truth in them.

This time she volunteered to let me know if and when she was in contact with Jeanette. I lingered, but she quickly picked up on my discomfort in the heat and offered to walk me to the door. Or, I walked her as she clung to my arm with brittle fingers.

"Not a day goes by that I don't question that decision," she mused. "They say when you have a child, all of your concerns are thrown out the window because you have just one concern now. Then again," she reasoned, "everyone in this home was placed here by their children, except me. I had to come here on my own." She paused to reflect on that decision. "I don't know which situation is sadder."

On my way out, I once again stopped by the front

desk and spoke to the attendant. She was trying to find order to a pile of paperwork and it looked like the pile was getting the best of her.

I interrupted her efforts. "Excuse me, is there a way I could leave a small gratuity for the staff for taking such great care of my aunt?" I asked.

"Why that is very thoughtful of you," the woman beamed.

"I'd like to leave it for the attendant I asked about earlier."

The beam got a little duller.

"Oh, okay. Well, you can leave it with me."

I took some of the cash I had on me to bribe the gossip blogger and started to hand it to the woman, but then had second thoughts and awkwardly pulled the bills back.

"Maybe I should just write a check," I said to the woman.

"However you prefer," she said icily.

"Tala…" I said, "…what was her last name again?"

SOCIALIZATION

The coincidences were too numerous to justify using that word anymore. People and places were integrally linked in a knotted mess that I had little hope I could ever untangle. I decided to focus on the connection of the nurse at the convalescent home. The fact that she hadn't shown up for work in days without an excuse was further proof that something was amiss. Still to be decided was whether she was coercing Jeanette or in collusion with her. Either way, I knew if I found Tala, I would find a path to Jeanette.

I gave the job to Badger. With my interview fast approaching, I couldn't risk pulling a disappearing act at work. Presence was an important quality for senior leadership and an empty office was not the ideal way to project an image of serious engagement in my work. And although the interviews would grant me ample time to meet and discuss my qualities and ideas with the decision-makers, there was a necessary pre-step I had to take if I had any chance of succeeding.

"Socialization" was the new buzzword at the office.

With so many new ideas and initiatives being pitched at once and so little mental "bandwidth" (and will) to process them all, leadership demanded they hear about each pitch on an individual basis before the actual meeting. The reason was clear: no one liked to be taken by surprise. This resulted in a mini-campaign of sorts, often off the calendar, for which you were expected to make the rounds to the various offices of the decision-makers for a quick "drop in" chat. You'd float the idea, get some initial feedback, and then agree that it would be good to discuss in the larger group. In the military world, this was known as "softening up the hill." In the corporate world, it was how people filled up their calendars. One meeting with ten people quickly became eleven meetings when you added in all of the individual ones.

I was so busy running around on my socialization work that I missed the breaking story—Nelson Portillo was wanted for questioning in the murder of Morgan McIlroy. She was apparently last seen with him leaving a restaurant in Silver Lake. The police had a school photo of the Portillo boy and despite the menacing words "Wanted for questioning" emblazoned over it, the kid still didn't look like he could kill another human being. There was no mention of Jeanette in any of the articles.

I foolishly put in a call to Detective Ricohr, and unfortunately for me, he picked up.

"What can I do for you, Mr. Restic? Do you want to confess?"

"No, but you have the wrong person in the Portillo boy."

"Now why would you know anything about that?" he asked, surprised. "Maybe *you* should be a person of interest in the girl's murder."

I hadn't thought through the phone call and was now getting myself entangled in a difficult situation. When I met with Detective Ricohr previously, I was not forthcoming with the details around Jeanette's disappearance because of some vague notion of client privilege, if there even was such a thing. But now having been summarily dismissed from my role as private investigator, so too was I released from any obligations to Valenti and his precious privacy.

"I may not have given you all of the facts when we first met," I confessed.

"I'm sure of it. Care to make amends?"

I told him what I knew—most of it, anyway. I explained the reason for meeting with Morgan in the first place and was clear that the missing girl I was after was, in fact, Valenti's granddaughter.

"You have a way of tangling with some pretty powerful people," he commented, but it sounded more like a warning than anything else.

I purposely avoided mentioning the original payment Hector made to Nelson's brother. I knew how quickly this would be misinterpreted as further proof of Nelson's potential guilt. And, I conveniently left out the part when Nelson tried to run me over, and the time he tried to escape out the window and then stood me up in the Rally's parking lot. Reviewing all of the stuff I left out of the narrative made me half-wonder if Nelson should be a suspect after all.

The other big piece that was conveniently left out

of what I told Detective Ricohr was any mention of Hector Hermosillo—the knife fight in the street and the prior arrest for murder in 1963. From what I knew about Detective Ricohr, he wasn't your typical cop. He was a pragmatist and didn't follow the easy route. But despite all that, I withheld the details about Hector because reasonable or not, cops tended to latch onto things and not let go. The last thing I wanted was the full weight of the Los Angeles Police Department to come down on my little magician friend. He didn't deserve that kind of treatment.

"I'm only telling you all this because I have met with the Portillo boy and there simply isn't any way he could have done what you are saying."

"I never said he did," Ricohr corrected me.

"Come on, Detective, his face is plastered all over the news. No one is going to split hairs when they see his mug in connection with the girl's murder. Right now, in the eyes of the public he is already guilty and it's only a matter of bringing him in for his punishment."

"You can't base police work on a 'feeling' someone has for a suspect after meeting them for five minutes," he chided, but his heart clearly wasn't in it. He was a decent soul and he was a better detective. "So you think the girl's murder is connected to the disappearance of the Valenti girl?"

"I do. There's something deep running under all of this that I haven't yet figured out. It could be about money."

"It often is. This Gao Li—he sounds pretty motivated to get back at the old man."

"Very motivated. His family hasn't had the best of

experiences with Valenti, to say the least. That shouldn't surprise anyone. Most people who deal with Valenti come out on the short end."

There was a brief pause.

"You still holding some anger toward the old man?" he asked me straight out.

"I may hate the man," I told him, "but not enough to do what you're implying."

My word seemed enough for him and he let it go.

"Why hasn't the family contacted the police?"

"Publicity."

"That sounds thin," he ruminated.

"Or selfish."

"Or both. I could alert my colleagues in Missing Persons, if you think that would help. We don't necessarily need the family to file a report if we think the girl is in danger, but it doesn't make it easy without the family's involvement. Especially this family."

I told him that it might do more harm than good. I didn't want to spook Jeanette by having her face plastered all over the news along with Nelson's, and provoke her into doing something drastic. It was also an unnecessary risk to Ricohr's career.

"What does that mean?" he asked.

"What are you, five or seven years from retirement?" I asked back.

Detective Ricohr and I shared the golden handcuffs also known as a "secure retirement." The last thing he needed was to be run off the force because someone with a lot of money and influence didn't like the way he handled the situation.

"We'll do what's right," he answered.

"Keeping this out of the headlines is the right thing to do."

Detective Ricohr processed the information and came to the same conclusion.

"There's nothing much I can do about the Portillo kid now," he said. "Maybe I was a little hasty but let's remember, he is the last person to have seen the victim alive."

"Other than her killer," I amended.

"We'll see about that."

"I'm going to prove you wrong," I told him, feeling my oats.

"Listen, pal," he fired back, "I'm letting it go that you lied to me when I first approached you about the girl's murder. But I am going to be very clear right here and now—if you pull that again, I am not going to be in a forgiving mood. You learn anything about anyone, you call me first. And if I hear otherwise…."

"There'll be hell to pay."

"Fuck off," he said and hung up on me.

THE SILENT SCREEN

I caught Jeff Schwartzman as he was about to leave the office. By the way he bustled about and didn't make much effort to actually settle down for a second and speak to me directly, I got the sense he wasn't in the mood to make time for me. It wasn't but a day or two ago that we were best friends, united in our work to bring home his daughter. Now I was the guy with the clipboard in front of the grocery store—if he didn't make eye contact then he wouldn't have to stop and sign my petition.

When faced with people in a rush, I have the annoying habit of slowing things down to a glacial pace.

"There was one thing…I, uh, wanted to…talk to you…about."

"Sure, but I'm in a bit of a rush so if it's quick, then let's walk and talk," he suggested, and assumed I would be in agreement because he hurried out of the room before I could answer. I didn't move from the spot where I was standing and patiently waited for him to come back. It took longer than I expected but he eventually reappeared in the doorway and put on his best annoyed impersonation. "Okay, what is it?"

"Did you ever get ahold of your daughter?" I asked.

"I did not. But I am not sure how that is any of your concern," he replied, pushing his way into his office and closing the door behind him. "I thought you weren't helping out on this anymore."

"So are you and the old man on speaking terms again?" There was no way he could have known that unless they were. My suspicions were confirmed when I looked back at the blank screen where the now-silenced video installation was supposed to be.

"Yes, it's common that family members talk once in a while," he said, taking on a snarky tone. Jeff seemed to jump between two personas—the Average Joe from the Valley or the High Society dabbler—depending on his current standing with the old man. By the way he kept addressing me like a servant, I assumed things had been temporarily patched up between them.

"Why the rapprochement?" I asked.

"I don't have to answer your questions," he told me again but didn't make any move to kick me out. "You're a very aggressive person. And I'm not sure I like it." He was slipping back into the kid from the Valley.

"How much do you know about what's going on with your daughter?"

"How much do *you* know?" he shot back.

"Plenty," I calmly replied. "She placed the article in the gossip blog."

I invited myself to one of the chairs and made him listen to all that I had learned over the last couple of days, including the connection between the nurse from the convalescent home and the clinic where Jeanette had her baby. He reluctantly sat opposite me and silently listened, though he did check his watch several times to remind me that he was a busy man and had places to go. Jeff didn't let on whether any or all of what I was telling him was new information.

"Are you finished?" he asked.

"Almost. Have you spoken to Mr. Li lately?"

"No, but I plan to," he answered.

"I'd like to be there when you do. I have some questions of my own that I want to ask him." He didn't acknowledge the request and overall wasn't as responsive to reasoning as in the past. The reconciliation between him and Valenti was more pronounced than I had originally guessed. "Jeff, it's time to go to the police. This is no longer an affair of the family. Murder is involved."

"Trust me, I understand the gravity of the current situation," he replied noncommittally.

"The number-one goal is to bring your daughter home, right?"

"Of course."

"Well, the best way to do that is to let the authorities help. They have the resources at their disposal. They can cast a net a lot farther and deeper than what you or I can do."

"Plastering her face all over the news sites?" he asked with a trace of contempt.

"Now is not the time to worry about decorum. That stuff is extremely painful in the short term but it fades a lot faster than you think. If she's made it this far I think she can handle a little ugliness in the media."

He sort of nodded but something made me wonder

if his original misgivings about the publicity were for fear for his daughter's humiliation or in fear for his own.

"I spoke to the detective assigned to the McIlroy girl's murder—" I said, but before I could finish, Jeff leaped to his feet, his face a contorted mélange of orange and red.

"You already went to the police!" he shouted.

"I didn't have to; they came to me."

"Well, you better not have told them anything."

"Or what?"

"That was not smart."

"You aren't exactly Mensa material, Jeff. And if you are getting your advice from somewhere, you might want to think twice about the source." It was a transparent warning that he was being manipulated. Valenti had his hooks back in him, but the question was, how deep? "I left out one other detail. Please sit down for two minutes and listen to what I have to say."

I conveyed my growing concern that Valenti could be the father of Jeanette's baby. I was careful not to make actual accusations, as I had no real proof, but the circumstantial evidence was starting to point in that direction. And I was worried that this could quickly escalate.

"That's outlandish," he commented without much indignation. If anything, he was trying to convince himself that it wasn't true. He stared absently at the pile carpet, his right eye blinking methodically as he thought things over. I let him stew in all of the ugly permutations and patiently waited for him to come to a conclusion.

"Listen, Mr. Restic," emerged magnanimous Jeff, that condescending creature prone to lecturing. "We can't let stressful situations lead us to make poor decisions...." It was a drawn-out speech of well-meaning but empty words. I smiled politely and thanked him for his time. He graciously walked me to the lobby door, but I refused his extended hand.

The man was a lost cause.

☺   ☺   ☺

I caught Meredith at home. She, too, had effectively been brought back into the family fold but at least she was honest about it. Unlike with her ex-husband there were no high-minded speeches to camouflage her real intentions.

"I'm going with which way the wind is blowing," she said, but it didn't sound like she was happy about it.

"Who's calling the shots?" I asked. She gave me a look that effectively reprimanded me for such a dumb question. "What is he asking you to do?"

"To go along with everything."

"Which is?"

She smiled. "That wouldn't be going along with everything."

"When did you know that Jeanette was pregnant?"

Meredith thought it through and it seemed like she was debating on whether to tell me the truth or not.

"About a month before she ran off," she finally answered.

"That's pretty late in her term."

"She hid it well," she replied but didn't feel like that was enough. "We don't have the best relationship," she added.

She didn't like the direction this conversation was going and decided to shift it away from her.

"Did they find the Portillo boy yet?"

"Not yet."

"I never thought he was the violent type but I guess you never really know what people are capable of doing, do you?"

I let that go unanswered until she looked up at me.

"You want me to play along to help you feel better?"

"Excuse me?" she shot back.

"You know that kid had nothing to do with Morgan's murder. But if you want me to talk you through it to ease some of your guilt I am happy to oblige. Is railroading Nelson part of whatever plan the family is cooking up?"

"It is not," she conceded. One thing I admired about Meredith was when I called her on something, she was big enough to acknowledge it. "And no, I don't actually think that boy had anything to do with Morgan's murder."

"Hire me," I said.

"What?"

"You don't believe any of this nonsense being flung around about Nelson Portillo being a murderer. And I don't get the sense you approve of whatever plan is being cooked up."

"I already hired you, didn't I?" She was trying to make a joke out of it to make it go away. I didn't let her.

"I can find your daughter. I'm close to finding her now. I need your help, Meredith." She nodded. I couldn't tell if I was actually getting through to her or if she was just buying time before shooting down my offer. "It's never too late to turn that relationship around," I added.

"You and me disobeying Dad?" she mused. "He would have a conniption."

"Let him."

She tilted her head back and stared out the large slider like she was watching a movie of some fictional world on the other side of the glass.

"Look at him," she said, pointing at Sami, who sat on the edge of a chaise lounge just outside the sliding door. I hadn't noticed him. He glanced in like someone pretending not to be interested in what was being said on the other side of the reflection.

"Does he sleep at the foot of the bed, too?"

"No," she said, laughing, "but I might ask him to. You're mean," she said after some reflection, meaning it as a compliment.

"Why are you shutting him out?"

"This is a family matter."

"So why am I here?"

"You won't be for long."

☺   ☺   ☺

I showed myself out. Meredith was my last hope, but even she couldn't resist the pull Valenti had on all connected to him. I took a moment to take in the cool air trapped under the thick marine layer before heading out on the long drive back to Eagle Rock. It roughly worked out that every three miles equaled one degree warmer on the thermometer. By that calculation it would be ninety-five in my neighborhood.

"Something is happening," a voice said behind me. Sami scraped through two dwarf palms. He remained close to the wall of the house and safely out of the sightline of the front windows. "Jeanette contacted them," he said.

It seemed to me he was taking an unnecessarily

conspiratorial tone, skulking in the shadows like a day-time robber.

"When?"

"Last night. Meredith got a call from her father. I don't know what they talked about but it was a long conversation. I tried to ask Meredith afterward. I didn't want to push it." But clearly he had tried. I waited for the response. "She told me it wasn't any of my concern."

"Who did Jeanette contact—her mother or the old man?"

"It sounded like her grandfather got the call," he said. "She is going up to the family house tonight."

"Jeanette is?" I asked, both elated at her potential return but wary of that same return.

"No, Meredith."

The family circle was tightening as Meredith and Valenti closed ranks. It didn't sound like Jeff made the cut. Fathering Jeanette apparently didn't qualify for full membership benefits. Jeff would be strung along like the stray following the wagon train to California. He'd never get a seat in the carriage but I think he was content with that arrangement. It was a better situation than the one for interlopers like me and hangers-on like Sami, who were shut out completely, left off at some depot in Topeka.

Sami wasn't taking it very well. He lingered among the prickly palm fronds as if afraid any movement would slice open his bare skin. He had foolishly led himself to believe he'd earned his way in. All the free booze and morning romps and promises of financial support had lulled him into believing it was real. He looked at me with plaintive eyes as if my sensible car was his last ticket out and last chance to catch up to the train.

"If I learn anything, I'll call you," I said, which sounded very much like an empty promise. I reflexively glanced up at the bank of windows above him. This sent him reeling.

"Did she see me?" he stammered.

Before I could reply he retreated into the stand of drought-tolerant plants and out of sight altogether.

THE FINAL DAYS OF THE GAO LI EMPIRE

The dismantling of the empire that Gao built was executed with methodical precision. This was not a job for pyrotechnic experts and their molar-rattling blasts. This one called for meticulousness, like an army of ants tasked with the dismemberment of the unfortunate cricket who had wandered into its path. While one piece was cut away and carried off, six more were loosened for their eventual removal. It was clean, tidy, and cold-hearted.

The opening move was, on the surface, nothing more than a random event. But in isolation they would all feel that way, until you strung a few together and started to get the feeling that there was some grander force choreographing each move.

Throughout the week I watched as Proposition 57 emerged from the bowels of the *Times* local section and rose into a big story. Local news sites suddenly featured polls dedicated to the issue. On my commute in to work and back home it seemed like every local radio was featuring the story with both proponents and opponents giving their side. There was big money behind the blitz and although the slant was fairly even, with a slight tilt in favor of the NO supporters, it felt bigger than anything Gao and his cohorts could muster.

I texted Claire during a break in a meeting: "PR machine in full swing. Yours?"

Her response spoke volumes: "We're on lockdown."

When the PR plan is underway you don't want any interference from your own ranks. The word had gone out to the troops. This was clearly coming from Valenti's side.

Gao himself was featured in several debates and interviews for both TV and radio. At once he was anywhere and everywhere and consistently with the same headshot. I realized later, as he must have after it was too late, that he walked right into the trap. The free publicity was a boon for his cause, which he greedily took advantage of at every turn. But he did not realize that his visibility was the goal all along. He needed to be recognized before he could be cut down.

The breaking story came just in time for the evening news on Thursday. Helicopter footage showed the dilapidated roof of the Victorian in Alhambra with a long line of police streaming into the front door of the house. The street was cordoned off to allow a string of ambulances to come and take the "residents" of the house to a properly sanctioned medical facility. The news outlets alternated between three sets of footage on continuous loop: the overhead shot of chaos and traffic jams, the image of a hysterical Chinese mother wheeled out on a stretcher while a female EMT carried a swaddled baby in her arms, and the arrest photo of the impassive-faced woman at the helm. She looked dour in person and downright grim in her mug shot. It wasn't long before someone conjured up the name, "the Baby Mill."

It was a compelling package of heartache—crying mothers, crying babies, crying relatives—and outrage: traffic jams, baby tourism, and longer traffic jams. It was all building to that one moment when two images juxtaposed against each other would serve as the coup de grâce. It happened early the next day, right in time for the morning news, when that now-familiar headshot of Gao Li was placed next to the truly unflattering mug shot of the mastermind behind the Baby Mill. That image alone sealed his fate.

It was a masterstroke of manipulation. Gao was a minority partner with a meaningless stake of less than five percent in a company that owned a series of properties across the Inland Empire. But despite this tenuous connection to these illegal activities, he was effectively implicated in a grander scheme. It made great fodder. Here was the scion of a respected Chinese-American family, the self-proclaimed standard bearer of the cultural heritage of a proud people, exploiting the weak souls longing for the opportunity to pursue a dream, the very dream his family lived. There were interviews with the victims who spoke from hospital beds about the conditions in the house and the price they had to pay so their poor child could have a chance at the American Dream. Gao followed up one grand blunder with more missteps in his foolish attempts at damage control. Proclamations that clarified his limited involvement in the operation went unheeded. Vitriol and attacks on Valenti cast him in a bitter light. Valenti may have dug the hole, but Gao jumped in and shoveled the dirt on top.

Jeff waited for the upstart to be slain and dragged through the streets before entering the fray to stand over the body and proclaim his indignation.

"I am disappointed and upset regarding the revelations surrounding Mr. Li," the prepared statement read. "As a citizen of the great multicultural city of Los Angeles, a longtime admirer and supporter of Chinese art and culture, and as a parent myself, I can no longer in good faith support Proposition 57."

No one seemed to question how pulling his support from the proposition was in any way connected to activities associated with the birthing clinic. In the end it didn't matter. Jeff had successfully maneuvered his way back into the winner's circle.

The gnawing thought I couldn't get to go away was a feeling that this was the plan all along, and that I was an unwitting participant in helping it come to fruition.

☼   ☼   ☼

I had a meeting with Gao on Saturday morning, but it wasn't planned and it didn't involve two willing participants. I caught him coming out of his "office" at the sign-less storefront in Arcadia. The noodle shop was continuing its brisk business and the brassiere shop its drawn-out decline.

"You got some balls, man," he said as I approached him in the parking lot. Three of his buddies were with him and were waiting for the thinnest of pretenses to start trouble. "Don't worry, I'll get him back."

"No you won't," I told him and it seemed like he knew it.

"This is probably another one of the old man's games," he said. "We stomp you and then get arrested for assault," he said after some thought. "It might be worth it."

The last thing I needed was to get my ass handed to me in an Arcadia parking lot because someone thought they were getting back at Valenti.

"I'd rather you didn't," I said. "I don't work for Valenti and this isn't some kind of trick."

"Then maybe we just stomp you anyway for fun." He laughed and his buddies laughed with him. I tried to join in but they stopped laughing when I started. "What do you want?" Gao asked me.

"Can we talk? There are questions I can't answer but you can."

"What's in it for me?"

"Absolutely nothing," I told him truthfully.

Perhaps my honesty struck a chord because Gao waved his friends off and together we crossed the boulevard to a coffee chain on the opposite side. The air conditioning inside was five degrees colder than the standard and the music three clicks louder than it should be to have a conversation. We sat in the corner to escape both.

I asked Gao to fill me in on the proposition and the impetus behind getting it put on the ballot. He effortlessly slipped back into campaign mode and all the flowery language that came with it. He spoke of heritage and cultural integrity. Away from the social club and the historical society, the banter fell particularly flat. "Social fabric" sounded especially tinny over iced lattes with an acoustic set playing in the background. Perhaps it was the setting or the recent events, but even Gao's heart wasn't in it. I let his diatribe peter out to its unconvincing conclusion.

"Tell me about the business angle," I asked.

A different person than the one who sat down at the table began speaking. It was the voice of an ambitious young man who spoke with conviction. It was the first truly genuine interaction I had with him.

"It's all about the condos," he told me. "Chinatown is the next wave in the downtown revitalization. It's hipper, closer to the freeways, sits over a new park, and you can walk to the train station. But there's no housing. It's just a bunch of two story dumps with live-chicken stores on the ground floor. You can't be renting a place out for three grand with rooster shit under you," he said, laughing. "We've had our eyes on that end of Chinatown for a while now. Hell, you can walk to a Dodger game if you wanted to."

"Who's we?"

"My investors," he clarified. "Then we get word that Valenti wants to put a museum there. I'm thinking, hell yeah! White folks love that art bullshit and it will give the place culture, which just means higher rent to me. We already had some pieces of property and were working on others but kept running into Valenti."

"He had the same idea."

"Trust me, there was plenty to go around. But he started making it difficult for us."

Valenti didn't want to share in the spoils that would result from fabricating yet another cultural center in Los

Angeles. Each had pieces of what the other wanted but neither side wanted to budge. Valenti's tactics for leverage were more advanced and had more weight behind them than Gao's limited capabilities, "so the idea of the proposition was born."

Gao smiled like the kid who was the first to solve the math problem in class. His was an infectious smile, and I couldn't help sharing in the triumph at such a brilliant and calculating stroke to get the best of Valenti.

"It's a shame we didn't get to see it through," he said and the smile faded. He shook his head, like an old man ruminating on his life's one big regret. "That stupid lady."

"Did you know what was going on in the house in Alhambra?"

"Do you know how many properties I have ownership in? Do you think it's possible to know everything that goes on in them? I am a landowner, not a priest."

"So you did know," I told him.

Gao laughed the laugh of someone getting caught.

"You're such a dick, man."

"I know I am. But I am also right."

"Maybe you are and maybe you aren't."

"Did you know Valenti's granddaughter was staying there?"

"I didn't," he said. "Not at first, anyway." Gao explained that he got a call a few weeks back from a stranger who told him that he had a famous person's family member at the home. "They were vague but kept hinting that there was money to be made in it."

"Was it a man or a woman?"

"A woman," he answered but didn't have anything more to add. "I wasn't thinking too clearly on the call."

"What'd you tell the caller?"

"I strung her along to try to pump her for information but at the end I just told her I wasn't interested. And then as soon as I hung up I had the girl kicked out of the place. I panicked. The whole thing smelled bad, like I was being played. I was a mess thinking that any day it was going to come. You showed up last week and I thought that was it. But no cops were with you. So I waited and waited," he said, "but nothing happened. A few days go by, then a week, then nothing. I was relieved as shit. Until the other day," he added.

Gao had no warning that the raid was coming. Neither did he ever hear from the woman who had called him asking for money.

"Do you know a nurse who worked there? Tala something?"

"You find that fat Filipina, you let me know," he answered.

"Have you been looking for her?"

"Yeah, I'm looking for her," Gao grumbled. "The bitch set me up. Who do you think brought that problem into the house?"

I relayed the information Badger had discovered on Tala. She never showed up to work and her condo in the Valley was partly vacant, like someone who had left in a hurry. I had asked Badger how he came across this information, and he subtly told me she had left a window ajar and he had looked around a bit.

Gao couldn't mask how impressed he was that I had this information. I seemed to earn some points with him for it.

"Do you think Tala could have been the woman who

called me?" Gao asked.

"Maybe. But if all she wanted was money out of you, she didn't need Jeanette to be at the house. She could have blackmailed you with the threat to expose the illegal activities going on inside the house."

"Do you think she's connected to Valenti?" I let my silence serve as a response. "Fuck, man," he said like someone who has been played.

"One other link to Valenti," I began matter-of-factly, "is a murder from 1963."

Gao studied me.

"He killed my uncle Heng," he said flatly.

"Valenti was never charged with that murder."

Gao understood the underlying meaning in my clarification.

"*Allegedly*, his thug killed him."

"Why?"

"Because unlike my grandfather and unlike my dad, my uncle didn't let himself be pushed around. He stood up to them. And they killed him."

"What was it over?" I asked.

"It doesn't matter. Another stupid deal that one guy got the better end of and the other guy didn't like it."

"This upsets you—"

"Fuck yeah, it pisses me off. My grandfather took orders. My big-shot father took orders. Uncle Heng didn't take orders and neither will I." The statement was somehow equally defiant and yet full of resignation. Gao didn't want to be pushed around by Valenti and all that he stood for, but inside he knew that was exactly his fate. His anger wasn't necessarily toward Valenti as it was toward the family that disappointed him. Also in his anger was a fear that his own limitations would lead to a similar outcome.

"Does it upset you enough to concoct a scheme to lure Valenti's daughter in so you could finally get back at the man?"

He studied me with abject hatred.

"You never shut down that birthing clinic," I reminded him. "And this mysterious caller doesn't quite add up, especially since you never heard from her again. Now this Tala woman is missing and you apparently want her found but can't seem to do it. Gao, it all sounds like a wild scheme to get back at Valenti that backfired and now you are covering your tracks."

"You're wrong," he said.

"Why did you allow what was going on in the house? You clearly knew what they were up to."

"Why would I do that?" he replied incredulously.

He humored me as I tallied up the litany of moral and ethical reasons. But I could tell right away that he didn't believe in any of them. It was all just words.

"Let me ask you something," he said. "What did you, or I, do to deserve the life we got today? I'm sure you have a nice house in a safe neighborhood." Not nearly as nice a house or neighborhood as yours, I thought to myself. "You have a decent job that doesn't require you to work very hard but still pays you good money and benefits. Good healthcare, retirement package?" he continued.

My attempt to guilt him was having quite the opposite effect.

"You probably have a couple of kids going to some private school and playing all the sports they want to."

It had been assumed that I had children so many times lately that I was starting to believe I actually did have my own brood. I was at the point of actually giving them names.

"Have you ever asked, 'Why us?'" Gao paused but not so I could answer. "Why do we get all this and not someone on the other side of the world? Are we that much better than them? Think about it. The only difference between us and them is that we were born on this soil and they weren't. Say what you want, but I'm at least giving them a chance. The same one we got."

In his odd way, the clinic was his only chance to even the score.

EVERYTHING'S ROSES

It struck me later.

I had stopped off at the office to catch up on work and on the drive home I took the surface streets back to Eagle Rock. The normal route involved a series of short jaunts on multiple freeways and at this time of day, taking the full brunt of traffic jams from multiple interchanges was not wise.

I wound my way over to the river and took Riverside up the western shore that skirted Silver Lake and then Los Feliz. Before fully entering into Griffith Park I crossed over the interstate at Colorado and then traversed the river and came into the backside of Glendale.

This section of Colorado Boulevard was stuck in another era, when it was the main route for hundreds of thousands of tourists coming to Los Angeles. Old motels with colorful names and even more colorful signs crowded long stretches. Many were flower-themed and played off the Rose Bowl, even though it was a good seven miles from here. I imagined the disappointment when a family of four from Akron drove all the way to

Los Angeles to the Roses Motel and found out what it actually was. The signs were now rusted in spots and the swimming pools were mostly filled in with concrete.

I had driven this street many times and always wondered how the motels stayed in business. The freeways that flanked Colorado had long drawn away any sort of tourist traffic and yet a good portion of these roadhouses remained. They had to have some sort of trade. Prostitution, I imagined, was a mainstay. But what about a young couple on the lam?

I quickly ruled it out. A newborn had to attract a lot of attention. And the couple couldn't have much in the way of resources. Jeanette didn't have a credit card. According to Meredith it was Valenti's attempt to raise a blue-blooded cheapskate. Perhaps Nelson had some money but it was probably not enough to pay for an extended stay at even the cheapest of these motels.

It all led to the suspicion that they were staying for free at a friendly residence where they could remain undisturbed. As I progressed along Colorado from Glendale into Eagle Rock proper, I went through the list of possibilities. Neither Jeanette nor Nelson had many friends, if any at all, and even if they did, those friends would have parents who most likely would not be willing participants in these sorts of shenanigans. Relatives were another idea that I quickly ruled out as far as Jeanette's side—no one would cross Valenti, not even Jeff's family. Nelson's family was a distinct possibility.

And that's when it struck me. They were meaningless words when I first heard them, just the utterances of an annoyed neighbor with a crabgrass problem next door that threatened to invade his perfectly groomed turf. The home was not being cared for and was bringing down the property values of those around it. He hoped I was there to do something about it. I remembered the house looking unkempt, bordering on abandoned. But then the neighbor's words said otherwise.

"They're not home," he told me.

Sheila Lansing had mentioned that she was a reluctant resident of the convalescent home. Such people often hold onto their past lives on the slim hope that they will someday be able to return to them. The empty house served as the perfect hideout.

As I reached my street I quickly made a U-turn and headed back to the freeway that would take me to Pacoima.

☼   ☼   ☼

I could barely hear the doorbell over the whine of the leaf blower from the neighbor next door. I stepped back off the front stoop and watched the curtained windows for any sign of movement, but none came. I then walked the perimeter of the house just in case the occupants were prone to fleeing, but on this day I hoped they wouldn't because the heat was excessively oppressive.

At the back of the house the yard was in even greater need of maintenance than the front. The dirt was like powder and coated my shoes in a thin film. I found the garbage cans around the side of the house. The fact that they had contents confirmed there were people living in the house. The existence of several used diaper bundles convinced me the occupants were those I was looking for.

"Can I help you?" asked an irritated voice.

The nosy neighbor held the silenced leaf blower like a shotgun.

"You know the people who live here?" I asked.

"Who are you?" he replied.

"We met before, remember?"

"Yeah, but who are you?" he persisted.

"I work for the original owner. The people staying here aren't supposed to be."

"No kidding? They're squatters? But they seemed so nice."

"Is there anyone else staying here with them? Maybe another woman, a little overweight, dark?"

"Nope, there's none of that going on here," he said defensively. His mind clearly went to a darker place than I implied. It felt like the neighbor still felt protective of the young couple. I decided to ease off lest he stir something up before I could talk to them.

"Well, I'll swing by later to see if they're home," I said casually.

"Hey," he called after me, "don't go getting them into any trouble." He wagged his finger at me. "They're good kids, you know."

"I know," I waved back and returned to my car.

I drove around the block and parked farther down the street, where I still had a good view of Sheila's house, but wasn't in a direct sight line of the overly protective neighbor. I didn't want him to see me and bring the local police down for questioning.

MAN LEFT IN CAR

I was a case study for why you should never leave your dog in a parked car. Even with the windows rolled down, the temperature inside was well over one hundred. I had a half-filled water bottle from a previous purchase that was warm enough to make sun tea. I futilely tilted the visor to keep some of the sun off of my face, but I didn't want to completely obstruct the view of the house and so I was forced to get the full brunt of the rays. An hour in, I hit a point of woozy bliss where the body is covered in a sheen of perspiration and the breaths are short and metered and hypnotic. With every passing car I angled my head to catch the slightest of breezes, which were as refreshing as a tall glass of ice water. After about the fifth one of these I kept my head in that position leaning against the doorframe. That's when I saw a set of eyes staring at me from across the street.

It was Nelson.

The adrenaline shot through me and I awoke from my lethargic state. His body started to lean, and I knew he was going to try to make a break for it.

"Kid, don't make me run. It's too hot," I pleaded. His eyes hung with me but his shoulders slowly swung around. "Come on, you couldn't outrun me in a million years."

He tried anyway.

I flung open the door in pursuit and fell flat on my face. My knees had buckled on the first step. The asphalt burned my palms and the tender skin on my forearms. Scrambling to my feet, my head swirled from the quick movements and from the heat off the pavement. For a moment I thought I might vomit.

"Will you stop?" I shouted, but Nelson had no intention of obeying my command. I was more annoyed than anything because despite the head start he hadn't made it very far down the street. And now I had to run, jog maybe, to catch up to him.

Nelson fumbled with his cell phone. He was a slow runner, slowed more when trying to text and run at the same time. My head cleared somewhat and I gave pursuit. I got within five feet of him long before he reached the intersection, and by the end of it he was so gassed that I briskly walked up behind him and horse-collared him to a halt.

"Stop with this nonsense, already," I said and wiped the prodigious amount of sweat off my hand that came from the back of his shirt. "Who are you texting?" I asked but didn't wait for a reply. I snatched the phone out of his hand and read the latest text: *Don't come home*. I didn't have to read the recipient's name because I already knew it was Jeanette. "Nice," I grumbled and handed him back the phone. "Let's go talk inside. I hope you have air conditioning in that house."

The living room was mired in an early 1980s remodel. The coffee table and TV console were made of lacquered blond wood. The floral-print wallpaper bubbled in spots and was starting to peel at the corners near the popcorn ceiling. It brought back memories of my parents' living room and getting a lecture for missing curfew.

"Listen, kid, I meant what I said before. I want to help you. If I didn't, don't you think the cops would be here right now?"

Nelson wasn't buying it, and I didn't think he ever would. He spooked Jeanette with the text he sent her, and if I had any hope of her ever coming back I was going to need him to help.

"Give me your money," I demanded. Nelson looked at me like I was mad. "Come on, give me your money. Don't tell me you guys are broke already?" I shook my head. "That rules out that option. Jesus, this is a mess."

It was the first step from a persuasive selling technique called "controlled drowning." The idea was to present the subject with several scenarios that all ended in locked doors. By gradually building on each hopeless scenario you could then dangle a solution that they never thought existed. The technique was undoubtedly developed by former Black Ops specialists.

I built an airtight case for gloom. They didn't have enough money to last a week. They didn't have friends or relatives who would be willing to help them. And then add the unavoidable fact that the authorities wanted him for questioning in a murder case. Eventually they would track him down.

"I didn't do anything to her," he cried. He tried to elaborate but the words stumbled out in an incoherent babble. The boy rocked in the chair.

"All right, take it easy. I know you didn't have anything to do with it." I let him come a few steps back from the edge before giving him another shove. "The detective on the case seems like a reasonable guy, but you never know with cops. They're a stubborn bunch and they got one and only one suspect—you."

"But I didn't do it," he said.

"Sure, but these guys' job is to close the case. That doesn't necessarily mean closing it with the guilty party going to jail. We just somehow have to convince these guys that you are innocent," I said but shook my head like what I had just uttered was a next-to-impossible task.

"How's the baby doing?" I asked. I needed to ease into this part lest he completely shut down. "What's his name?" I asked, even leaning back in the sofa to ease the tension.

"Holden," he muttered.

"*Catcher in the Rye* fans?"

"Yeah."

"Great book," I lied. I thought it was great when I was too young to know better. "You left the father out of that decision, huh?"

"What do you mean?" he asked, looking a little hurt.

"I'm sorry. I assumed you weren't the dad."

"He's mine," he stated.

"Nelson," I said, leaning back in, "I have no doubt that you can and will be a great father, but you're not *the* father."

"It doesn't matter who it is," he said after a moment. It sounded like even he didn't know the identity of the father.

"No, I get it. But obviously the courts won't see it our way."

That one had a greater impact than I thought it would. I had successfully maneuvered the kid to the point of total despair. It was time to bring him back. What was supposed to feel like a moment of triumph instead made me feel ashamed.

I convinced him to meet Jeanette and the three of us would contact the authorities. I would hire them a lawyer and be with them every step of the way. Nelson nodded his head in resigned acceptance of my plan.

There was a knock on the front door. We looked to each other for an explanation.

"Jeanette?" I asked.

"I doubt it," but there was hope in his voice.

"Could be the neighbor next door," I said.

We were both wrong.

"Hello," said Detective Ricohr with a smile, but there was nothing cheerful about it. "Can I come in?" he asked as he crossed into the living room.

Nelson stood by the couch as the detective and the local police streamed into the increasingly cramped space. Through all the chaos Nelson never took his eyes off me.

"Sit down, son," Detective Ricohr instructed. "This wasn't Mr. Restic's fault. Not intentionally, anyway." He turned to me. "I took a gamble and put someone on you. I had a feeling you knew more than you let on."

We all walked out together into the late-afternoon

sun. It sat low on the horizon and felt hotter than it should. The police activity attracted many onlookers from the surrounding homes, including the neighbor on the left. I avoided his gaze but I knew it was directed at me. I was getting tired of disappointing people.

☼   ☼   ☼

Detective Ricohr rode with me on the long drive back to downtown. We were like a couple of travelers forced into intimacy on an oversold bus. There were no TVs to distract us and nowhere at all to escape.

We talked about anything and everything—the sectarian violence in the Middle East, which neither of us really understood, the inanity of LA's freeway system, for which major feeds crossed each other and somehow didn't have connectors, the wild idea to have the concrete-encased LA River return to its natural state. Detective Ricohr was more of a revealer than me, and I heard all about his various ailments, his divorce from twelve years ago, and the three kids from the marriage. Two things we did not talk about were the weather and the murder case.

I dropped him off on First Street in front of police central headquarters.

"What's going to happen to Nelson?" I asked.

"We'll just talk to him for a few hours and see what we can get and then send him home."

"He probably won't say much."

"That's what everyone thinks. Until they actually get in there."

"No, I just don't think he knows much about the girl's murder."

"You said before that you thought the murder and the old man's missing granddaughter were connected."

"I think the Valenti girl has the information, not this kid."

"Do you know where she is?"

"If I did, I wouldn't be hanging with you."

"What's he paying you, if you don't mind me asking."

"Nothing. He fired me."

Detective Ricohr mulled that over. He let two late commuter buses, with their roaring engines and plumes of exhaust, pass by.

"If you find the girl, do you find my killer?"

"When I find the girl and talk to her, your killer should become very clear."

"You hope."

"*You* hope," I corrected.

"We both hope." He headed into the building.

"Detective," I called him back. "I'm sorry for not telling you everything ahead of time. And you may not believe it, but I was going to call you after I had spoken to the kid."

"Save the apology for later," he said. "I suspect this won't be the last time you disappoint me."

Tired as I was, I headed in the opposite direction of my house and drove out toward the Westside. I stopped at a diner just off the 10 Freeway and sat in one of the booths by the window. I picked at a tuna melt and fries but mostly I watched the heavy stream of traffic funneling on and off the freeway. There was something hypnotic about it. After the third time I was asked about a water refill, I got the hint and decided to give them their booth back.

Time never moves more slowly than when you're trying to kill it. I drove aimlessly around the side streets but that was only good for a half hour. I did a couple of tricks of randomly picking destinations and then driving there and back a few times like a runner doing track work. Finally I gave up and drove over to Nelson's house and parked in one of the few open spots on the street.

I don't know how long it took because I dozed off a few times but eventually a car appeared and parked in the narrow driveway. Nelson squeezed out of the passenger door and headed for the house with his tatted-up brother at his side. If I factored in all of the wasted time in and around any visit to a police station, the fact that Nelson was home before midnight was a bit of a miracle. Detective Ricohr had kept to his word.

I wasn't finished with Nelson. He was my one link to Jeanette. I got out of the car, though not entirely sure what I was going to do to get past his brother and overprotective *abuelita*, never mind what I would say to him to get him to talk to me again. In that moment of hesitancy, I watched Nelson and his brother walk toward the front door and I marveled at the unspoken support emanating from the backs of one person walking next to another in silence. There was no steadying hand, no arm around the shoulder. The brother didn't even hold the door for Nelson. But the young man was back with his family and that was a good thing.

I got in my car, fired up the engine, and headed out for the long ride back to Eagle Rock. The black sedan waited for me in front of my house.

A DIFFERENT KIND OF DYING

I parked in the garage and came out the side door. Hector waited for me on the walkway. We silently made our way inside, and he stood patiently in the center of the living room while I turned on some lights and opened the windows to let in the cooling night air.

"They got another email," he told me after I stopped buzzing around the room. I made a move to sit down, but Hector made no move at all, so I remained standing. "They want more money."

"How much?" I asked.

"Three million."

This time I sat down and thought it over. That was quite a jump from $45,000. "I assume it came from Jeanette?" He nodded. "Did you see the actual email?"

"It was sent to Mr. Valenti. I heard him talking to his daughter and Jeanette's dad."

"What did you mean by 'they' wanting more money?" Hector shrugged his shoulders but I could tell he had some ideas. "The police found the Portillo boy," I said, and explained exactly how they found him, but the mention of the boy didn't register with Hector. "Who do you think it is?"

Hector deferred to his boss. "Mr. Valenti said if it was either of them he'd crush them."

"Either of whom? Meredith and Jeff?"

"He told them when they came to the house."

It was not a surprise that Valenti had suspicions about his daughter and her ex-husband. He was innately suspicious of everyone when it came to money. I wondered if he thought they were in on it together. Individually, they both had the motive, and if I thought about it enough, I could imagine each attempting something like this, or trying it together.

"Sit down," I instructed. "You're making me nervous." Hector shot me a look but eventually took a seat on the couch. "What do you think about this?"

"I don't know. It's not my business."

"Then why did you come here to tell me about it?"

"I thought you would want to know."

That reason made little sense. He had already pushed the limits of his relationship with Valenti when we were working together, but the act of coming to my house smashed all of those limits in one stroke. He was betraying the confidence of the family to someone whom his boss had dismissed. Valenti valued privacy above almost anything and this impropriety would have repercussions beyond Hector's mere dismissal from the job he'd held for nearly fifty years.

"You know something that you're not telling me."

"I'm not lying."

"I know you aren't but you're also not telling me everything. You're concerned about something. Otherwise, you would never have come all this way in the middle of the night. What is it?"

"I told you everything."

"When are they supposed to pay it?" I asked.

"Tomorrow night. We're gonna get the instructions tomorrow in the morning on where to bring the money." Hector paused a moment. "I'll be delivering it."

"Is the family bringing in the police?"

"No," he answered, but it didn't sound like he agreed with that decision. From my limited time with Hector, I never got the sense that he was a card-carrying member of the Police Benevolent Society. He was a man who preferred to settle his own disputes in a manner of his choosing. The fact that he had some misgivings about leaving the police out hinted further that he was concerned about something.

"Are you worried about what might happen to you tomorrow?"

Hector shifted in his seat into an even more upright position.

"I can handle myself," he said coolly.

"Then what is it?"

"I think she's dead."

The words hit me hard. It was one of those conclusions you ruled out because internally you weren't prepared for it.

"Why do you think that?" I wanted Hector to defend his opinion so I could shoot it down.

"I saw the email," he admitted and stared at the floor. "They printed a copy and left it on the desk. I shouldn't have read it."

"What did it say?" I asked.

"It said that if Mr. Valenti didn't pay the money that he would never see the baby alive."

"That's it?" He nodded, but I didn't understand how that sentence meant Jeanette was dead. "I would never bring my baby into it," he explained before I could ask. "A parent doesn't do that."

And there I was again, not understanding the realities of being a parent.

"She's dead," he stated. As if even his convinced mind wasn't quite ready to abandon even a trace of hope, he added, "I think."

"What does the family say?"

"Mr. Valenti is afraid like me."

"Why do you say that?"

Again there was a hesitation. After decades of subservience, it didn't come easy to talk so openly about his boss.

"After his daughter left," he began, "I saw him in his study. He was crying. I never seen him cry, not for anything. It didn't look like him. He saw me and I thought he'd yell at me or worse, but he just stared and cried. He told me he couldn't lose them."

"Do you know who the father of Jeanette's baby is?" Hector shook his head. "Your boss was very close to his granddaughter, wasn't he?" It came out crasser than I intended, not that any degree of tact would have mattered because once the allegation registered with Hector, he leapt to his feet and his right hand flicked for his pocket. "Take it easy," I said. He stared at me with distant eyes. For the first time in our relationship, I was actually afraid of the man. "Hector, listen to me. You didn't come here because you thought I was out to get the old man. You want to help him and you think I can help you do it. And I'm trying. I want to bring

Jeanette home as much as you do and almost as much as Valenti."

Hector hadn't moved and it was unclear if any of the things I said had any effect on moving his hand away from the nifty little number in his pocket. I wanted to get him talking.

"If I'm going to help you, I am going to need some answers. You and Valenti have a pretty tight bond— I can see that by the way you defend him. I need to know why."

The forever-young man with young-man-like reflexes and a younger man's temperament seemed to dissolve in an instant. I could now see the grays beneath the shoe-polish black. I felt the aches in his lower back. I saw the tired eyes of someone who had seen too much over too many decades.

"I should have died," he said, but the death he was referring to was not the one I assumed it was.

Hector recounted the events leading up to the night in 1963 when Gao's uncle Heng lay dead on the street in the Alpine District. To my surprise he came right out and admitted to killing the man. "I stabbed him in the stomach and he didn't fight any more," he stated. Hector looked straight at me when he said it. I searched for signs of remorse and found none. But it wasn't like he was proud of the deed, either. There was a strange detachment from the retelling of the death, a matter-of-factness that escaped my own sensibilities.

The actual events were mundane to the point of being clichés. Hector was working for the construction company that Valenti owned. It was his first real attempt at a stable earning life. The job was a small development where a corner of a block was being converted into row houses. Hector explained that there were troubles immediately with the job. Their work was periodically vandalized, their supplies constantly delayed, their tools stolen. "That was the worst part," Hector explained, "because we had to bring our own tools and without your tools you couldn't work. It cost a lot of money to replace them. It was money out of our pockets."

Everyone was certain that Heng Li was behind it. It wasn't much of a secret, as his cronies taunted the workers whenever they could. They often hung around the job site, and sometimes Heng himself joined them. There were a few skirmishes between the two groups but nothing very serious came out of it—that is, until the night of the murder.

Hector was out with friends in some of the dives around Bunker Hill. This was long before the hill became the glittering home of my corporate headquarters. At that time the Victorian neighborhood was a shell of its former self with seedy establishments haunted by lost souls left over from another era. The birth, death, and rebirth of communities comprise a never-ending story in Los Angeles.

The couple of pops with friends turned into an all-night bender as they crawled from jukebox to jukebox and cruised the tunnels under the hill in a borrowed convertible. At some point in the night, Hector crossed the line of no return and decided to power through with a few more drinks and then get himself sobered up before his morning shift started. Home in East LA was too far away, and no one was of any mind to drive him out that way. They continued on until the group lost its steam, and Hector had his friends drop him off at the construction site, where he found a pile of wrapping from roofing tiles and used that as a makeshift bed to sleep off the bender.

He was awoken by sounds of shattering glass. It was near sunrise and Hector had to orient himself, and his woozy head, to the commotion coming from no more than fifteen feet away. He saw Heng smashing a set of newly installed windows with a roofer's hammer. Hector confronted him and the two faced off.

"I guess I could have took off," he reflected and then summed up why he hadn't. "We're all just stupid, I guess."

Hector pulled his knife, Heng took a swipe at him with the hammer, and then it was over. All along I waited for Valenti's entrance into the narrative. And now that we were at a point when a man lay dead, I was both confused and a bit dubious about the whole thing.

"I don't understand. How did Valenti save your life?"

"He showed up to the job site an hour later and found me. I was crying—crying like a little baby. This guy was dead and my life was over. He asked me what happened, and I told him."

"Then what?"

"He left, told me to stay where I was and not do anything. He came back twenty minutes later with the boy's father."

I made him repeat that last part. I had heard it clearly enough but it didn't sink in. He confirmed that Valenti brought the elder Li to the construction site and showed him the poor boy's body and explained what happened. Hector apologized to the man, but the old developer didn't say anything to him. He and Valenti eventually walked away to talk in private. Valenti returned alone and gave Hector instructions.

"We were supposed to call the police and say that Heng had threatened Valenti with a hammer and that I came in to protect him and that's how the boy died."

"Why didn't you just tell the police the truth? It wasn't murder the way it happened." His look was enough of a reply to make me sorry I asked. In those days there wasn't a lot of faith in the police or the courts to listen to reason, especially when minorities were involved. He was right in assuming his chances were slim to none.

"Either way I was supposed to die that day. Either get killed or get sent to jail," which in his world was just a different kind of dying. "And he saved my life. I owe him."

THE CORNFIELDS

I was five minutes late for the rendezvous with Hector the next night because Pat Faber had dropped by my office as I was leaving to see if I was getting nervous about the upcoming interview. That wasn't how he phrased it, but I could tell that was his intention. I told him I looked forward to the competition and I was going to "rise to the challenge," but the hope for a quick chat was not in the cards. Pat reflected on the many defining points in his career where he similarly rose to the challenge—and won. After several minutes of my telling him how invaluable his perspective was, I finally extricated myself from the tedious discussion so I could go meet Hector.

His sedan was parked in one of the three slots infront of the Phoenix Bakery in Chinatown. I had to park on the street. The sweetened air around the bakery was so pervasive that each breath felt like another layer of sticky film was added to my throat. It made me thirsty, but it just could have been that I was nervous.

Hector got out when he saw me and was not pleased

with my tardiness. I knew enough to skip an apology and just get down to business.

"Badger here?" I asked.

"Right here," came the reply as Badger stepped out of the shadowy area by the restaurant next door. He wore his amber sunglasses despite the moonless night and this desolate part of the city being one of the darkest in the area. I could barely see anything beyond an arm's reach, but he maneuvered easily and proffered a conciliatory hand to Hector.

Earlier that day, Valenti had been instructed to deliver the money to a spot in the middle of the Cornfields, a long park that used to be a railway yard just east of Chinatown. Hector was the natural choice to perform the deed, but Valenti didn't know about me being involved, and Hector did not expect Badger to be there as well. He stared at Badger's outstretched hand with visible contempt.

"No hard feelings, *Paco*," said Badger, doing his best to provoke an already annoyed man.

Hector looked to me for an explanation.

"Another set of eyes can't hurt," I told him. He didn't like it but he didn't have much of a choice as we were an hour away from the appointed time. "Do you have the money?" I asked Hector because that felt like the right thing to do, though the idea that he would forget the money on the night of the drop was absurd.

Despite all that, Hector moved around to the back of the sedan and opened the trunk for us. Three million in cash was surprisingly smaller than I anticipated. I envisioned a forklift and a heavy pallet but instead got a medium-size duffel bag. But it was heavy—very heavy.

For a moment while holding that bag, I felt the warmth and comforts of being a millionaire. And I had an impulse to bolt. I heard Badger grunt behind me. Even Hector cast a sly, little smile. This was the moment when someone would casually suggest the money getting lost and the three of us running off to Mexico. Hector squelched that dream by snatching the bag from my hand and replacing it in the bed of the trunk.

We went over the plan while standing there in the bakery parking lot. Hector would deliver the money as expected. He was going to enter the south side of the park, off of Spring Street. Badger, with his WW II battleship binoculars, would position himself on the Gold Line platform toward the west end of the park that offered an elevated and unobstructed view of the entire area. I would wait in my car on the north side of the park on Broadway. This also offered an elevated view of the area as the land gradually sloped upward toward Elysian Park, the 110 Freeway, and Dodger Stadium. But it also was an exposed area with very little cover and almost no human activity at night. I needed to be careful lest I was spotted before the drop could be made.

The idea was that once Hector delivered the money to the requested spot, Badger and I would watch the area for the individual who picked it up. Part of me wished it would be Jeanette, despite the complications that would involve. But deep down I knew that was an unlikely scenario. The more logical outcome would be that whoever picked up the money was behind her disappearance, and possible death. We weren't going to let that person out of our sight.

"I'm on point," Badger explained. "I can reconnoiter

from the shield wall on the platform." Badger was using an inordinate amount of military lingo for my taste
and I could see it was grating on Hector as well.

"If you screw this up," Hector warned, "I will
kill you."

"Listen, chief, I know what I'm doing."

"He does this for a living," I added, but it had little
effect on changing Hector's overall mood.

"You brought him," Hector reminded me. It was
clear that in Hector's mind, the threat toward Badger
also included me. We all wanted to do this right, but
Hector was the only one who really had something
to lose.

We tested our cell phones for good coverage and
established a three-way text as a communication chan-
nel. As Badger's "ROGER THAT" text buzzed in, Hector
stomped off to his sedan and drove away.

Badger set off to the train station on foot, while I
got in my car and drove the short distance to a spot just
on the edge of complete desolation where the industrial
buildings ended and the run down to the LA River began. There was a bus stop inexplicably placed on this
stretch of road like a last stop to nowhere. Even more
perplexing than its existence was the fact that four or
five people were waiting in the glass structure. It looked
like a perfect cover for me to watch the proceedings in
the park below.

I shuffled over to the bus shelter and mingled
among the riders. There were two old Asian ladies with
canvas sacks full of leafy vegetables; one also had what
appeared to be a plastic bag of chicken feet. The other
three were Latino laborers either coming from or on

their way to a nondescript manufacturing center on the other side of the river. They had the tired eyes of those on the eternal night shift.

The tie and jacket were left behind in the backseat of my car but I was still odd man out in my pressed pants and recently shined loafers. And while the coterie of late-evening riders watched with longing eyes for any signs of the bus emerging from the flickering neon of old Chinatown, I was fixated on the black pool of park below me, a flat mass broken only by evenly spaced lampposts and their white circles of light.

My cell phone hummed with a text from Badger: "IN POSITION." I replied that I was in position as well, but a third confirmation never came from Hector. Not that I expected one, but it would be better if we communicated at a high level during this maneuver. I regretted not giving my "over-communication" lecture before we disbanded from the bakery parking lot. It was ingrained in the corporate world that there is no such thing as too much communication. This pervasive "feedback loop" resulted in in-boxes filling up with "FYI" emails at a five-per-minute clip. But in a scenario like the one we were in, knowing everything was vital.

It was still five minutes from the appointed time when Hector was to deliver the duffel bag of money, but that didn't keep me from checking my watch every thirty seconds. Of all the people in the bus shelter, I was the most impatient. They had the resigned looks of people waiting for a ride that was perpetually late.

I spotted Hector.

He was a solitary figure in a white shirt that flared up as he passed under each pool of lamplight. He moved with purpose despite the heavy load slung over his shoulder. I scanned the park but saw no other activity. He was close to the drop point, a garbage can near the center of the park.

"LOCKED ON TARGET" came the text from Badger.

Hector approached the garbage can and let the heavy duffel slip from his shoulder into his hand. He placed the bag on the ground right on the edge of the cone of light from a nearby lamp. I could barely make out the dark lump from this distance. Hector turned and headed back toward Spring Street.

Around me came the rustling of bags and shuffling feet. Barreling down on us was the 762 bus to Boyle Heights, a brightly lit number with a few ghost-like passengers and a driver cast in shadow. As my shelter-mates formed a makeshift line, I turned back to the park and looked for any activity. There was none. I strained my eyes on the spot where Hector left the bag but couldn't quite make out if it was still there. I shielded my eyes from the glare of the oncoming headlights but still struggled to see anything in the darkness. The whine of bus brakes squelched behind me and the doors exhaled to let on the passengers. After a moment came a voice.

"You coming?" asked the driver. I waved him off without turning around. "There ain't no other bus than this one," he came again.

"I'm good, I'm good," I said.

The driver brought the doors in and pulled back into the street, leaving a plume of exhaust that got caught up in the shelter.

"TARGET IS IN PLAY" came another text from Badger.

Again I scanned the area but didn't see anything. I replied, asking for clarification.

"HAS THE BAG MOVED?"

"TARGET IS IN PLAY" repeated the text.

"FOR FUCK'S SAKE HAS THE BAG MOVED?" I rattled back.

Badger replied with one word: "AFFIRMATIVE."

I saw nothing, just the same dark landscape with the white polka dots. But then something moved in and out of one of those dots. I trained my eye on the next one and after a moment the figure appeared again under its harsh light and then slipped back into the black. It looked like a man pushing something. My eyes jumped ahead and waited. He came into view again and this time I got a better look at him. He wore a long, dark coat and pushed a shopping cart filled with something a good foot above its sides. He moved back into the darkness.

It gave me time to type my question: "THE HOME-LESS GUY?"

"AFFIRMATIVE" came the response.

This time, Hector chimed in: "DON'T LOSE HIM."

That's when I got nervous because I didn't know if the man was part of the plan to pick up the money or if he was just a homeless guy who found a bag full of money left in a park and decided to add it to his collection of street detritus. The thought of Valenti hearing about the latter scenario sent shivers down my spine for what he would do to Hector who in turn would do it to me.

I caught sight of the man and his cart in one of the pools of light. He was following the path toward its north-side exit. I calculated how far the park entrance was from me and what I was going to do when he walked through it. Three more times he passed under the light and now he was no more than 200 feet from leaving the park. I watched the final pool of light for the man, but he never appeared. I waited and still nothing.

"LOST THE TARGET" Badger texted.

And I fell into full panic mode. My instinct was to run down there but I didn't want to alarm the man or whoever might be watching him besides us. I instead walked purposefully in his direction, trying not to call too much attention to myself.

My phone buzzed with the incessant texts from Hector wanting to know what was happening. Each one grew shorter than the last. I envisioned him hammering away with each text and getting angrier with each send. I resisted the inevitable as long as possible, which was to reply with the truth that I lost the man.

I pulled up the phone to answer his question and typed three dreadful words: "I DON'T KNOW."

The phone then fell out of my hand. I looked around, disoriented, and realized I had run headlong into the homeless man's shopping cart. We looked into each other's eyes. My gaze was rooted in fear. His look was rooted in schizophrenia.

"Motherfucker," he muttered and pushed the cart like I was not standing there. I jumped out of the way but the front wheel caught my foot and left a track on my polished loafers. The man continued on down the street in the direction where I had just come. Rather than tail him directly, I grabbed my phone and crossed the street to the sidewalk on the opposite side, giving him a little distance.

I wanted to text the boys that I was on his tail but couldn't risk being distracted or being spotted doing suspicious activities. I crossed in front of a small Catholic church with a well-lit Virgin Mary and an Italian social club next door. The homeless man was maybe forty feet in front of me. I kept him in my peripheral vision. We continued on for a few more buildings and then he stopped in front of one of the cars parked on the side of the road. I stopped also, thought better of it, and continued on at my original pace.

I came up even with the man and casually glanced across the road just in time to see him hand the duffel bag over to someone inside the car. In return, he was handed something that looked like money.

I kept moving but I heard the car roar to life. It swung out from the curb and into the middle of the street to head in the opposite direction. I made myself as small as possible but kept my eyes on the driver of the silver compact, the same shitty car that Nelson used to try to run me over.

The Filipina nurse—both her pudgy hands gripping the steering wheel and her eyes trained straight ahead—roared past me.

I took off down the street toward my car. Fumbling with the key, I got the engine started and sped after her. But the street was just an empty stretch of asphalt with no red taillights to follow. The twinkling lights of Chinatown ahead were a false siren.

As I passed Bishop Street, I caught a pair of taillights out of the corner of my eye. They turned right and out of sight. I put both feet onto the brake and came to an angled stop. I reversed without checking and luckily found open road. I pulled onto Bishop and hoped I hadn't made a mistake.

Zooming up the street, I ran one stop sign and then another and finally caught up to the taillights. As I followed the car onto the on-ramp to the 110 Freeway, relief and excitement washed over me like a cold shower—the silver compact was idling at the entrance and waiting for an opening to pull onto the freeway. I slowed so as not to get too close but managed to pull out my phone and send a very simple, reassuring text: "I'M ON IT."

A WOMAN'S LAUGH

It was easy to tail her in the moderate traffic heading back to Pasadena. Tala didn't change lanes, which allowed me to stay in the same one without fear of getting too close or slipping too far back. For three steady miles there was a consistent two-car distance between us.

I took that time to fill in the details to Hector and Badger. Hector texted back that he was in his car and coming my way. Badger was far from his own car but he would do the same without delay.

We drove all the way to the end where the freeway funneled us onto the surface streets leading into Pasadena proper. We turned left at California and moved our way through the leafy neighborhood before turning south toward Hermon. I began to wonder if Tala knew I was following her because she could have gotten off at an earlier exit on the 110 to get where we were now. I slipped back to be extra cautious.

Tala took me on a journey of endless turns and loopbacks to the point where it felt like we were going in circles. Without any visual guides in the dark night, namely the looming San Gabriel foothills, I had no way to tell if we were heading north or south. Each new street looked like the one we just got off.

But then I began to pick out landmarks—a familiar billboard here, a recognizable street name there—and I started to feel less like a raft adrift at sea and more like a canoe with one oar. I finally spied the unmistakable glow of Dodger Stadium at night and I realized that we were headed back into the city, back to the very area in Chinatown we had just left.

I followed the compact toward the concrete bridge into the back-door—once the front-door—entrance into the city. I eased up on the accelerator to put even more distance between me and Tala's compact. We were the only two cars on the street for a good half mile. As we glided over the crest of the bridge, I straightened the car for the wide-open stretch downhill and called Hector with my free hand.

"Where are you?" he asked in place of any sort of greeting.

"I'm still following her. We're heading back into Chinatown, just crossing the bridge now."

"What street?" he asked.

"Spring."

I heard the squelch of tires over the phone as he turned his sedan around in the opposite direction. Over the roar of his engine, "I'm coming now."

I trailed the compact down a wide, empty street fringed with industrial buildings. They were windowless structures with iron-faced front doors. Even with a great distance between us, I still felt exposed. My headlights must have been like beacons in her rearview mirror. I slipped back even farther despite the fear that I would lose her.

That was a mistake.

Suddenly, the two red orbs were no longer. The street that lay ahead was dark and empty and the numerous cross streets had little to no activity on them. I couldn't tell which street the compact pulled off on, if at all. Panic set in and I was convinced that I had gone too far and quickly turned around. I zoomed back from where I came but soon, much too soon, encountered the bridge and realized I'd backtracked too far. I spun around again, arcing too wide and careening into the curb. I floored it and rumbled down the street in the original direction.

The corporate hack in me immediately ran through a series of excuses why it wasn't my fault that I lost her. I was ashamed at how easily this instinct came. And I was amazed at how good the excuses were, given such a brief gestation period. All began with "we," the classic maneuver to position failure as a shared responsibility. *There were a lot of things we could have done differently....*

A lot of things we couldn't anticipate....

The excuse diatribe would end on a positive note, a look forward at the next steps to get us back on track. Unfortunately that was where I came up blank. There was nothing I could think of to do. This was the last step.

I pulled over and let the weight of that conclusion settle in. Hector couldn't be far from me at this point. It was only a matter of minutes and I put my phone onto my lap as I waited for the expected call. The street was refreshingly quiet. Sometimes you have to go to the heart of the industrial complex to find true peace. I sat there and marveled at the lack of sound and thought of nothing. It was incredibly peaceful.

I saw movement in the darkness. Or, at least I thought I saw something. It came from the cross street off to my right. I used the old trick of looking out of the corner of my eye, which somehow made it easier to see things in the dark. I sat there, head tilted toward the steering wheel, hopeful that a flicker of movement would appear in my peripheral vision. None came, but I felt driven to search further and put the car into gear, then turned onto the street.

This street had no parking restrictions and therefore was lined with vehicles serving as makeshift homes for unseen occupants. Back windows were shaded out with towels and newspaper to provide a modicum of privacy to the sleeping souls behind them. Most of the cars didn't look like they were in shape to drive more than a mile but in truth all they had to muster was a thirty-foot hop to the other side of the road on street-cleaning days.

One car, though, stood out.

Tucked between a van and a grime-covered station wagon was the compact I had been searching for. I cruised past it toward the end of the block and shut off my lights. I glided into an open slot at the end and parked in a fire zone as a wave of relief washed over me—there would be no need for collective excuses tonight.

I texted Hector and Badger my location and took a moment to scan the area. When I had passed the compact it didn't look like Tala was inside. She had to have slipped into one of the industrial buildings, but I couldn't be sure of which one because the few windows on this near-windowless block were all dark. I got out to investigate.

Any movement would easily be noticed on this quiet street. I couldn't risk spooking Tala into flight so I looped around to the back of the buildings. This was a wider block because of the loading docks that drove the activity during the daytime. I made my way down the alley, hugging the sides of the building to avoid the light cast by the occasional lamp. At about the spot where the compact was parked on the opposite street, I noticed a solitary window on the second floor with a dim, orange light emanating from inside. I drifted toward it like an insect to a porch light.

I clambered up onto the loading dock. Two large, rolling steel doors and a regular-size door with an impressive-looking lock formed an impenetrable entrance. Shading the entire area from the relentless southern exposure and from the occasional thunderstorm was a roof jutting ten feet out from the building. It was also a good ten feet above me. Having humiliated myself before in attempts to touch the rim of a basketball hoop, I searched for another means of reaching the roof.

Back in the alley I found a rusted length of pipe and dragged it back to the dock. I leaned the pipe into the corner where the roof met the building and then wedged the bottom end against a pillar. I monkey-crawled up the pipe but was winded a third of the way up and had to rest. I pressed on until the back of my head touched the edge of the roof. Unfortunately I hadn't thought ahead to figure how I was going to move my grip from the pipe onto the edge of the roof without falling to a very painful landing below. With my forearms growing numb, I knew I had to stop deliberating and just try. I uncrossed my legs and let them dangle below, nearly launching myself off the pipe. With one hand on the pipe, I twisted around and threw my other hand toward the roof and grabbed hold of the edge. A sharp pain greeted my palm, which soon grew damp with blood. I donkey-kicked my leg up to the edge and pulled myself on top.

I was gassed. I sat on the roof in a dazed stupor, my head swirling in oxygen-deprived blood. I glanced up and made out the view to the north with a clear shot of the park and then understood the importance of this building's location relative to the drop zone. That seemed to give me a jolt of energy and I got to my feet to face the next hurdle, a far less challenging one, which was to get to one of two windows above me. The one on the left looked like it hadn't been opened in thirty years. A pale light behind it illuminated the chicken wire in the glass. The darkened one next to it was open and my only way inside.

I positioned myself below the open window and made the very doable, bottom-of-the-net leap to reach the sill. I gritted my teeth and pulled myself into the room. On the floor was a pair of binoculars a third of the size Badger used for a similar purpose earlier that night. The presence of the binoculars led me to wonder if more people than just Tala were involved in the ransom. My mind leapt to Jeanette but I dispelled that notion—for now, anyway.

With the filing cabinet and desks and papers piled on top, it appeared to be an office of a still-operating business. I remained at the foot of the window and strained my ears for any sounds coming from the other rooms. It was as quiet as the street outside. The only sound in my ears was from my own heartbeat thumping away. I made my way to the door, careful not to trip on anything and call attention to my presence.

The hallway was empty. The only light came from the room to my left. I stood for what felt like twenty minutes but was just a single minute. I took out my cell and texted Hector and Badger.

"I'M INSIDE."

The reply was immediate. From whom, I wasn't sure, but the phone buzzed in my hand and broke the silence in the hallway.

I thought I heard a click. I waited, my eyes fixed on the door a few feet from me, but nothing happened. I detected movement inside, or rather, the faintest shift in the half-light as something, or someone, passed in front of the light's source. I concentrated on my breathing but nothing could suppress the sounds emanating from my chest. It felt like anyone outside on the street could hear my panicked attempts at air.

The barrel of a gun slowly emerged from behind the doorjamb, then the pudgy hand that held onto it. Tala stepped fully out of the room. She seemed focused in the opposite direction toward the stairwell that led below. It hadn't occurred to her that someone might be behind her.

I could have done several things—rush her while my position was still unknown, turn back into the darkened room and leap to safety onto the loading dock roof below—but I did nothing. These were options somewhere in the recesses of my mind but they never fully emerged.

As if sensing something behind her, she slowly turned and faced me. She looked around with a slightly perplexed look. I watched her go through the thought process as she put the pieces together—someone found me, it isn't the police, he is alone. The gun rose ever so slightly, the grip firmed up on the butt.

There was a whir of black behind her as a figure approached. As it passed the lit room, I saw Hector's face illuminated in the yellow light, then move back into the shadows. He came up behind her with mechanical, almost robotic efficiency. His arm went over the one holding the gun, there was a glint of silver from his knife, and then I heard something that I thought sounded like a woman's laugh, but wasn't. I watched how effortlessly the arm with the gun came down. The hallway flashed bright, followed by a roar as the gun discharged a bullet into the floorboards. I covered one of my ears, trying desperately to get at the dull tone drilling inside my head.

It looked like Tala wanted to sit down, to rest a spell after a long day of work at the hospital. Hector obliged by hooking one arm under her shoulder, which was now black with her own blood, and gently lowering her down. The extent of what he had done hit him as he stared at his own stained hands. She sat there on her folded-up legs in an awkward pose on the floor. One arm propped her upright but strained under the weight and didn't look like it would hold much longer. A large pool grew rapidly around her, far quicker than I ever thought possible. I stared at the expanding ring and wished it would stop. It didn't.

The sounds that started coming out of her were a quiet plea that I knew would go unanswered. They were so feminine and fragile. And I fought the urge to rush to her side and if nothing else, just hold her in my arms, because I knew it was too late. Instead, I closed my eyes so I wouldn't have to watch it. But the sound didn't go away.

I'd never heard anything like that in my life and I wished to all's end that I never would again.

NO KIDS

Badger showed up a short time later and surveyed the scene. When he saw the body lying in the hallway, he calmly approached and felt for a pulse on Tala's neck even though by the way she lay there it was clear she was dead. He used the backs of his fingers, felt nothing, then rose and checked his watch. It felt to me like the moves of someone whose next move was to flee and pretend he was never there—no fingerprints on the skin, no evidence at all to place him at the scene. I expected him to request that Hector and I leave him out of the entire story we told the police. And I didn't blame him in the least. He had more experience than I did in what lay ahead for us and he was wise to not want to experience it.

"It's ten-forty," he announced. "We call 911 first but we call our lawyers immediately afterward. Let's make sure we have the numbers handy because this thing will go down faster than you ever thought possible."

Badger wasn't running, and I felt sorry for doubting him. He called 911 and told them the minimum amount of facts. It appeared the operator was trying to pump him for more information but he hung up. He then called his lawyer and filled him in. I took Badger's lead and called the only lawyer I knew, my ex-wife Claire. As a commercial real estate attorney she knew nothing about criminal law, but she was all I had. I also held this growing need to be near someone I knew and Claire was the closest person I had in all of Los Angeles.

I got her voicemail.

"Claire, it's me. I think I am about to be arrested. I'm in Chinatown so not sure where I will be held. Can you help?" Before I hung up, I felt the need to add, "Sorry to bother you with this. I'm in trouble."

Hector didn't call anyone. Badger and I pleaded with him, but he ignored our requests. After the few words he whispered when Tala died—"I only tried to stop her"—he refused to speak at all. I thought of calling Valenti directly but worried that would only complicate matters. Hector could have easily placed the call to the old man himself but he chose not to. I didn't know his reasons but I respected them.

Badger was right. The "mess" was on us faster than I thought possible. The siren wails grew louder with each passing second and soon were joined by heavy footsteps on the stairwell. Radio squawks joined the cacophony of sounds coming at us. Per Badger's suggestion, we sat together on the floor with our backs against the wall and our hands clasped over the tops of our heads. At least Badger and I did the last part. Hector joined us on the floor but his arms remained by his sides, his bloodied palms face-up in a resigned pose. As the cool-white glare of heavy flashlights danced in the hallways, I caught a brief glimpse of Hector's face. He looked drained and lost, and his cheeks glistened pink where he had tried to wipe the tears away with blood-stained hands.

☼   ☼   ☼

I never felt exhaustion like I experienced in the period that followed. I remember snippets of what eventually became a two-day ordeal, but they seem like scenes haphazardly cut together from several different movies.

There was an interrogation room that was as cold as a walk-in refrigerator. I recall pulling my arms in through my sleeves and wrapping them across my chest in an attempt to retain what little heat emanated from my core. I would have done anything for a shred of blanket so I could curl up on the corner of the linoleum floor and go to sleep.

I remember an odd combination of odors—pancakes and radiator steam—so strikingly familiar that a rush of memories from my third-grade classroom came back with such clarity that it felt like I was sitting in that second row again under the paper mobiles dangling from the ceiling.

And I remember a uniformed officer of pronounced age who escorted me in and out of rooms with the gentleness of a nursemaid. He had the saddest eyes I had ever seen and this look like he would one day walk out the front door and never come back.

I did a lot of talking over those two days but can't recall much of anything that I said. They asked the same questions over and over again, and even I grew tired of my answers and felt the urge to change it up just for the hell of it. If my responses failed to stop the repeated asking of the same questions then I assumed something was wrong with my answers. For a fleeting moment I even bandied about the notion of telling them that I was the one who held the knife and was ultimately the killer, but self-survival kept me from making that mistake. Not that they would have believed me anyway.

With distance from the onslaught of interrogations, it became clear that they weren't interested in me. It was in the questions they asked and in the tone they asked them. They spoke to me like a child, half-filling me in, half-asking me to fill in the holes for them. All of their questions revolved around the "how" more than anything.

How did Valenti come to hire me to find his grand-daughter?

How did I find out there were ransom notes?

How did the first payment happen?

They had Hector, but more importantly, they wanted the puppeteer manipulating the strings. They operated on the assumption that every murder follows a logical path, and this one followed a winding little road back to the old man himself. Tala's murder, and perhaps even Morgan's, were part of some conspiracy. Perhaps the murders weren't pre-planned but they were certainly deliberate. And I was just the rube they used along the way when it helped their cause.

After some time, a suited man appeared in more and more discussions and seemed to be on my side. He was introduced as my lawyer though I didn't recognize the face and was certain we had never met. But he clearly wanted to help me and for that I was grateful. I came to rely on his presence so much that when he left the room I had this instinct to run after him, lest he leave me behind and never come back. But he always came back.

On his last visit he led me through a maze of hallways and forms and ultimately deposited me into a parking lot where I was greeted by damp night air and the hum of air conditioning units.

Claire was there to give me a ride home. I didn't know where my car was—impounded in a lot somewhere—and I didn't have the energy or the sense to find it. We drove through the near-empty streets out of downtown and unwittingly passed the Cornfields park where this nightmare began. Not that I really noticed or cared. I was exhausted and felt detached from everything around me. I could smell the new-car leather and feel the gentle heat of the seat warmers but it didn't seem like I was actually there in the passenger seat with Claire as the city went by. Every now and then she told me bits of what she'd learned, like how Hector's knife had hit a hard-to-reach artery that caused Tala's quick death. I didn't speak, just let her words float over me.

We stopped at an all-night donut shop in Highland Park. It was expectedly empty at three in the morning. The lone worker manning the shift no one wanted shot us an annoyed look that signaled we were rudely intruding on the private world she occupied every night and every early morning.

We sat at a yellow Formica table in a booth by the window under the garish glow of fluorescent lights. We drank scorched coffee, and I forced myself to eat a fritter just to have something in my stomach. As the crappy coffee took its effect and the rhythmic ticking of the lights overhead provided a beat that I could fall in line with, I slowly started to feel okay again. I found myself listening to the subtle sounds of Claire drinking coffee, her bracelet rattling on the tabletop as she placed the cup back down. It felt good to be near her. But there was a vague emptiness about the whole thing. I was no closer to finding Jeanette, and the hope that I eventually would didn't seem like much of a hope at all. Lingering behind all of this was a question I never intended to ask but felt compelled to anyway.

"Why didn't we have kids?"

Poor Claire gave her best shot at a reason, but it was clear that she didn't have the answer either.

THE INTERVIEW

The job to lead the department was out of reach before the first interview even started. Because of the nature of our industry, the firm required associates to hold to strict standards of conduct in their lives outside the office. That didn't mean one couldn't cheat on his wife or screw a friend out of money. Those were considered private issues no matter how public they often became. The firm was more interested in official legal issues, such as a DUI, urinating in public, or getting arrested for manslaughter and conspiracy charges in a botched blackmailing scheme.

For a firm that was intrinsically risk-averse and for a job whose sole purpose was to keep the company from being sued, the idea that they would choose someone with so many questions around him was a dim option.

I knew Paul would make sure he brought my extracurricular activities to the attention of the key decision-makers in the hiring process. He wouldn't do it in such a straightforward way as, "Did you hear about Chuck?" No, he would find some back-door method like sending out a memo requesting any updates to the Code of Conduct Handbook or promoting a new study on recidivism of persons who have committed misdemeanors.

The idea of reporting to Paul made me shudder, and I let myself drift off with the daydream of quitting before it became official, but deep down inside I knew I wouldn't do that. I had it too good to be throwing it all away because I didn't like guys with ponytails.

I still had to go through the motions of the interview for a job I never wanted and now had zero chance of getting. But despite all of that, I wasn't ready to roll over. Perhaps it was all the unfinished business of recent events that increased my desire to see something through to its end. I was tired of all those unfulfilled reminders piling up behind me and couldn't face Jeanette's eventual addition to the list. Or maybe it was just that I despised Pat so much I wanted to make his decision to deny me the role as difficult as possible. Whatever the reason, I wasn't going down easy. .

The first round was with the recruiting representative from HR. And although I was four times her senior in the same department, protocol dictated that she kick off the interview slate. She showed up in a tailored business suit that looked new. I smiled internally at the act because in many ways this was more an interview for her with the future head of the department than it was for me as the potential future head. She needed to make a good impression and thus was more nervous than I was. I helped guide her through the standard list of questions and we got into a nice rhythm. It felt good to loosen up a bit on questions straight out of the manual I helped pen.

"Tell me about a time when one of your ideas was not adopted and how did you react?" was the question to probe on overcoming adversity.

"If you had to change one thing over the last five years in your career, what would it be?" was a way to get insight on someone's self-reflection tendencies.

My preparation for this portion of the interview was to drop key words from the job description in each of my responses.

"...foster a *collaborative* environment...build *integrated* capabilities...nurture *cross-functionality* between groups...."

The poor thing literally made check marks on her paper each time I used one of these phrases. By the end of it she was almost ready to shout, "You're hired!" I thanked her for her time and then commended her on a very well-run interview.

I didn't let this cream-puff session lull me into complacency. The interviews that remained would get successively more difficult and less predictable as I went through the day.

We transitioned out of the gobbledygook of HR into the business world with its own set of fabricated jargon. The important thing to remember was that the interview was not about me. The interview was all about the person asking the questions. If you could unlock them and answer accordingly, then your chances of getting hired were greatly increased.

So when the head of IT asked me how the firm's culture influenced results, I knew what he was really asking. The question reflected his concern that a stodgy management was slow to adapt with the times and spend money on new technologies.

"A firm that does not evolve constrains its long-term viability," I began. "The challenge is"—there are no problems, just challenges—"to make the hard decisions now, as unpopular as they may seem in the moment, that will pay off in the future."

I thought the man, with his ever-shrinking budget and zero respect internally for the thankless job he performed admirably day in and day out, was going to leap across the table and kiss me. I might have said nothing, but he found an ally.

I did this dance for hours and I loved every minute of it. It was as close as I could get to that feeling athletes have when the game feels slowed down, when they see every move before it happens. I was making shit up left and right and it all went down as easily as soft-serve ice cream. And with each interview I slowly began to convince myself that I might have a chance at this job after all.

During the lunch portion, I purposely avoided carbs and caffeine. I didn't need a post-sugar crash to mess with my rhythm. I ran into a little trouble at the two o'clock portion with the head of administrative assistants, when we got sideways on my approach to associate development (for dead-end jobs), but I quickly rescued it with a clever turn of a phrase involving "stepping stones" and "paths to career fulfillment."

The three and four o'clock interviews with the head of operations and chief compliance officer respectively were victories before they even began. It was as if they sensed when they entered the room that they were about to talk to the man who had the job. I didn't let hubris get the better of me and I battled in those sessions with equal vigor. By the time they were over I felt like I could go twelve more rounds.

The final interview was with Pat Faber. The room was now stuffy from the late afternoon sun pouring in and from all the hot air puffed over the last seven hours. I bounced out of my chair to greet him by the door. We each attempted to out-pump the other with a handshake, and I gleefully registered the disappointment on his face. He expected an exhausted man. Instead, he saw someone who was ready to uppercut him into oblivion. Pat rose to the challenge.

"What does failure look like?"

"A man who accepts things as 'good enough.' "

"What's the one thing you would change about yourself?"

"Nothing. The first step is recognizing your faults then figuring out how to succeed despite them."

"What would you change about me?"

"Ask easier questions."

"Why shouldn't we select Paul for the job?"

"I want to be selected on my strengths, not on another man's weaknesses."

They kept coming, and I kept knocking them down. I took the best he had, and Pat knew it. By the end of it he looked more tired than I felt. He leaned back and offered up one more, a true softball if there ever was one.

"What will be your legacy?" he asked.

All I had to do was come up with a pithy reply about generational change and throw in some anecdote to seal it. Victory sat right in front of me. But I didn't take it. I just sat there and said nothing. An uneasiness settled over the room. I detected a trace of glee as Pat watched me struggle.

The simple question had the effect of smelling salts under my nose. I was suddenly overcome with the clarity that comes from complete detachment. We were talking, after all, about a legacy of a body of work that had no meaning. And then I remembered Bob Gershon, the gentle giant who learned that fact too late in his career to do anything about it. I saw his face as if he were there in the room with me. I watched him disappear behind the elevator doors. Then I recalled the photo of a young Jeanette digging her toes into the sand. She was likely lost forever with no answers to explain why. And the entire thing became pointless.

One can fake it for only so long. I shook off my stupor and focused in on Pat.

"I probably won't have one," I answered, which was the first bit of honesty I mustered all day. "And if I were ever fortunate enough to have a legacy, I hope to God it wouldn't be for this job."

☼   ☼   ☼

I noticed it first on my way to lunch. And it was still there on my way back. Most of the black sedans parked in the loading zone in front of my building lingered for no more than the time it took to throw a travel bag into the trunk for the executive on his way to the airport. But this sedan sat idling, the tinted windows obscuring the occupant behind the glass.

I was foolish to let myself believe it was Hector inside there. I wanted to see if he was okay. I also had many questions to ask him. But his legal issues were far from over and there was no way he would be back into his old routine of driving Valenti around the city.

"Can we talk?" a voice called out as I passed by the car. It was Valenti.

I came back and joined him in the front seat. He picked up on my surprise at him driving his own car.

"I drove a truck when I was younger," he shot back. "I'm not that completely out of touch with the real world."

The air conditioner was pumping a steady stream of cold air that made the hair on my forearms stand up. As if sensing this, he lowered it to a gentle breeze.

"Anything I can do to help smooth things over at work?" he offered. "I could place a call."

Even Valenti's influence couldn't undo the damage I had done. I declined his offer. "I like to think I got myself into this situation and it's on me to get myself out."

"Still have that chip on your shoulder," said Valenti.

"How's Hector?" I asked.

"Hector will be fine." Then, appended, "legally, that is."

"Has he been released?"

"Yes, he is out but has some charges lingering that we can hopefully get cleared up soon." There was paternal pride in his voice. "We have the right folks working on it."

I didn't have a delicate way of broaching the subject of Jeanette and decided to just ask it outright.

"Have you heard from her?"

The man deflated. His only response came in the form of a barely perceptible shrug. Faced with an outcome he didn't want to accept, he seemed to be here as part of a last-ditch effort to find some scrap of hope to keep him from avoiding the inevitable. I was tempted to oblige but couldn't seem to piece together a lie.

"I'm sorry," I said instead.

He turned away from me and placed his hand on the shifter. I took that as the signal that our brief encounter was finished.

"Who's going to take care of this old man?" he asked absently.

All this talk about fortunes and inheritances and cycles of wealth suddenly felt insignificant. The powerful man was now an elderly man with elderly concerns.

As I stepped out of the car, he said behind me, "I'll always remember the last time I saw her. Never let that happen to you."

It was a personal admonishment framed as advice. But it was the worst form of advice—the kind given after it was too late to do anything about it.

I went back to the office and called Detective Ricohr. I was losing sense of why I made the decisions I did other than this one just felt like the right thing to do. I needed to know some things about Jeanette.

He called me back later in the afternoon. He was more cheerful than I anticipated. I had caused this man a lot of grief with my amateurish meddling. I would have swatted me away a long time before, but Detective Ricohr had a far deeper reserve of patience than I ever did.

"There was no evidence of the girl or baby in the building where the killing happened," he told me after the preamble about how he shouldn't be telling me this information, that it is still an ongoing investigation, etc. He was probably doing it for the recording machines at police headquarters. "And no evidence of her being at the victim's condo," he added, preempting my question.

"What's the collective view on the kidnapping?"

"There's some disagreement. Most think she and the Portillo boy were in on it all along, that it was some sort of blackmailing scheme. What they had on the old man no one is really sure. A minority think they were just two dumb kids duped into participating. In both scenarios we think she and the baby are dead. That's the one area where everyone agrees."

I thought that through but something didn't fit.

"You don't like it," he stated.

"I am not sure I know enough to like or not like it," I told him. "But it doesn't seem right."

"Not everything ties up into a nice little bow, you know."

"You're right," I agreed, as unappealing as those words were.

"Are you done?" he asked.

"I can't think of any other questions."

"No, are you done with the whole thing?" I didn't know how to answer him. It felt like there was more to do. My internal deliberation gave him his answer. "I didn't think you would be. This will fall on deaf ears, but don't be an idiot."

"I'll try not to," I said with a laugh.

"Seriously, don't be an idiot."

"That's sound advice, Detective."

"Make sure you take it."

A FAMILIAR SOUND

This time I came prepared.

I parked my car in an open spot fifty yards or so from the house. I brought food and water to last for some indeterminate length of time, enough backlogged newspapers to occupy my mind, and a blanket and pillow, although I didn't end up using the latter. For a day and a half I stewed in my car in the merciless heat and picked at the flaw in the consensus thinking around the blackmailing scheme. If Jeanette and Nelson were complicit, wittingly or unwittingly, why would she be the only one who had to lose her life?

In the time outside his house, I never saw Nelson but that didn't mean there wasn't plenty of activity. It mostly revolved around Nelson's brother, often accompanied by his grandmother but sometimes alone, coming and going from the house on an endless stream of errands, most of the time returning with arms laden with giant shopping bags of unknown contents.

Things settled down in the evening. The lights burned behind the curtains for so long that I thought no one ever turned them off. They eventually went dark sometime after midnight and stayed dark until a brief moment in the early hours when a light from somewhere deep in the house clicked on. The faint yellow spoke of insomnia or thirst or something else. It didn't last long and the house remained dark for the rest of the night.

I never went to sleep. I turned the car on once or twice to pump some heat into the cabin and to activate the wipers to clear the accumulation of dew from the front windshield. The city was remarkably still in those few hours before sunrise. A beautiful sun eventually inched its way in between the houses and lit up the side of my face. The wonderfully sad pink of an early Sunday morning spread over the neighborhood.

I watched the *abuelita* waddle out in a floral print dress and fake pearls and purse heavy with the words of God. Her son, reluctantly "dressed up" in black slacks and a white T-shirt, trailed behind her at a distance that conveyed a preference for doing something else with his free morning. I checked my watch—quarter to nine. Fifteen minutes until the service began. I placed a quick call, gave it a few minutes in case they returned home for some forgotten donation envelope, then got out of my car and pushed my stiff legs to the front door of the house.

My knock rattled the metal door like tin plates used to scare crows out of a cornfield. I didn't think Nelson would run but the delay in answering the door led me to doubt that assumption. Just as I was about to loop around the back, the door opened and the kid stood there looking disheveled and sleepy-eyed. He still had his pajamas on. I gently brushed past him before he marshaled any form of defiance. There was an unmistakable smell lingering in the air, something sour. I helped myself to the couch with the overworked springs. Nelson remained by the door, his hand still on the knob.

"Hey, what are you doing?" he started three seconds too late because I was already seated and had no intention of leaving. "You can't come in here. You'll wake everyone up."

"They already left for church," I told him.

"Oh," he said, looking around like someone trying to get his bearings.

"Why don't you sit down," I instructed. "I have a couple of questions for you."

"I already talked to the police."

He came and sat opposite me anyway.

"I know. I want you to talk to me."

"Why should I?"

"Because I asked you to." I spied one of the shopping bags in the corner. "What's all that?"

"I don't know," he replied, looking annoyed.

"Mind if I take a look?" I had no intention of getting up, but Nelson did and made a move to intercept me. It was the fastest I had ever seen him move. "Must be something important."

"What do you want?" he asked. He was getting his legs under him and stood over me in as threatening a pose as he could probably ever muster.

"Can you tell her to come out, please?"

"What?"

"Come on, kid, stop screwing around and tell her to come out here so we can all talk."

"She's not even here," he tried. "I don't know where she is."

"It's okay," said a soft voice.

Jeanette stood at the edge of the hallway. She wore

a nightgown that looked borrowed from an old woman and probably was. Her hair was loosely pulled together in a band and rested limply on her shoulder. Her eyes were heavy from interrupted sleep and spoke of a mother's weariness. Even her voice, made deeper from having just awoken, added on a few years.

"You're the man working for my grandfather?"

She was the only one who questioned my temporary job whose gaze didn't include a judgment with it.

"Right now, I only work for a faceless corporation. But yes, your grandfather hired me to find you."

"You found me," she smiled. "Now what?"

"Let's talk about it."

Jeanette joined Nelson on the couch. He took her hand in his to offer support but it was clear in the gesture and in the way she sat there that she was the one providing the support.

"So, tell me the plan."

Neither wanted to start but I could tell by their shared look that they had thought something out in fairly deep detail. It took some coaxing by me to get it out of them. Jeanette eventually took the helm and explained their next move, and that's when youth finally revealed itself in all its glorious stupidity.

They had some vague plan involving a cousin in Mexico and fifty grand they thought they were going to get to live off but didn't. They made it sound a hundred times that because, as they repeatedly reminded me, "Everything is super cheap in Mexico." Nelson had relatives to help with the baby and they could work and live some simple life and get away from the "meanness of people" in our city. Apparently, only happy, caring people lived south of the border. I let them blabber on because there was something charming about their irrational hope and the total conviction with which they expressed it. They were just a couple of knuckleheads too delusional to see the inanity of a "plan" that didn't deserve that name.

I led them to believe I would help them so that I could dissuade them from trying it in the first place. And the one thing I knew I needed to do to accomplish that was to not let them out of my sight. I threw out the hundred grand that Valenti had promised me and the idea that if I could collect it, then they could have it to help set up a life in the pueblo. That excited them far more than I thought it would. They latched onto the offer like it was the single solution to all of their troubles. They went so far as to strategize how they could help me get it. Jeanette could meet her grandfather to prove that I fulfilled my duty and then she could escape at a later date. We all agreed this was the best approach, and although I thought it was the dumbest idea ever uttered, I couldn't help but share in their excitement.

Jeanette got up from the couch and headed back down the hallway toward the bedrooms. Then I heard what her mother's ears heard before me, the soft gurgling and then the full cries of a hungry baby. Nelson and I continued the planning discussion and worked out the remaining details before we could fully lock it into place.

There was a knock on the door. Nelson went to answer it.

"Where is she?" a voice asked.

I looked over but couldn't see who it was.

"She's here," the voice declared. "I know she's here. The lady told me."

As I went over to investigate, I watched a hand reach in and push Nelson back into the room. Sami stepped through the doorframe. He kept one hand on Nelson's chest. The other held a rusty hammer that he let dangle by his side.

"Whoever you're looking for isn't here," I said but it didn't seem to matter.

Sami closed the door behind him and locked it.

"Where is she?" he asked again.

No reply could get him to stop asking the question. There was a serenity and distance in his eyes that was more unnerving than when I first stood under his penetrating gaze. He was talking to us but you got the sense he didn't even realize there were humans in the room with him.

I slowly moved in between Sami and Nelson, and even more importantly, between Sami and the back room where Jeanette and the baby were. It felt like the slightest of movements would upset whatever precarious balance Sami held in the doorway. I had to somehow get him out of the house, but having no physical skill to do that, I just tried talking him out. The words were meaningless; it was more the steady, lulling cadence that allowed me to creep toward the door.

Sami opened up his stance, just a little, but the meaning of the gesture was there—he considered letting me pass. I walked into the opening and crossed within striking distance of the hammer. I felt somewhat confident he was going to let me by but I couldn't really be sure. And the thought that I now had my back to him made me even more on edge, as a blow from that hammer to the back of my head could come without warning at any moment.

The lock moved easily under my thumb. I reached for the handle and slowly swung the door open.

"Let's talk outside," I said softly. Sami started to lean in my direction. "We'll be better when we talk out here."

He looked up at me and I believed I was finally starting to get through to him. His eyes had a flicker of life in them, a spark of engagement. His leg swung around and took its first hesitant step toward me.

Then that sound again from deep in the house. I heard it first. I watched Sami's right eye narrow like he was trying to reconcile the distant gurgle with the people in the room. Confusion crossed his face as he couldn't quite put it all together. I filled the silence with my dithering, just spilling out nonsensical words, anything at all to mask the sounds and distract his attention from what was emanating from the back of the house. It didn't work. The unmistakable cries of a newborn filled the room. Sami's head snapped around and his body followed with cold, sleek precision as he calmly walked in the direction of the baby's sounds.

I ran after him. It was the only time in my life that I just acted. I caught him outside Nelson's bedroom and threw my body into his backside. We toppled to the floor, and I rolled off his back and into the hallway wall. I reached out for the arm with the hammer and grabbed what I could. He jerked his arm back and freed himself from my grip but he also lost his balance and fell back into the opposite wall. Jeanette's screams filled the narrow space. Nelson came bounding down the hall. I barked an order but he was already ahead of me, dashed into the room with Jeanette and the baby, and slammed the door shut. The room was the only source of light in the hallway and the closed door cast a near darkness between me and Sami. I didn't wait. I threw myself forward to the spot where I thought he was. I felt a hard wall but I also got a piece of soft flesh. I clawed at it and anything I could. I felt something warm and moist which might have been his eyes. He wriggled underneath me. I tried to make myself as heavy as possible to keep him down. There was a loud thud and I found myself letting out an airless cough. My back suddenly felt hot and tingly. I gasped for a breath of air and although all the components for breathing were in motion, no air came in.

Another thud from the hammer crashed down on my back, this time lower and squarely on a bone. My mind became singularly focused on keeping his body close to mine. I somehow knew that distance between us meant more blows from the hammer but in more dangerous parts of my body. But with each swing, I felt myself being drained of what little energy and strength I had. My arms numbed from exhaustion. I held on but without any kind of force. I was slipping down. My eyes, now adjusted to the darkness, saw a form moving up and away from me. It made a swift, arching motion, the hammer slightly trailing.

Then the form jerked backward and a loud clap exploded in the hallway. Sami spun off his feet and stumbled down to his knees. There was barely a pause before he propped himself up with the hammer and got back to his feet. He struggled back into a striking pose.

And despite the window of escape, I remained in my position on the floor. The hammer squared itself for a blow to my head.

"Don't do it!" a voice behind me shouted.

It jarred Sami from his focus of crushing my skull. But he didn't drop the hammer. He stared at Detective Ricohr and the gun pointed at his chest. In the brief ten seconds of standoff between Sami and the gun, I could see the deliberation in his head and the eventual conclusion that his own life was much too important for him to let it end prematurely. He smiled and let the hammer fall to the floor.

BLACK ROCKS

The following couple of days were a flurry of activity involving a quick hospital stay and the interminable visits from members of the police. Claire came to see me a few times, but her face was only a brief respite from the parade of nurses and doctors and detectives that asked endless questions that I was often too tired to answer. Detective Ricohr came once just to admonish me for ignoring his advice.

"But I did listen," I reminded him. "I called you before I went into that house."

"And if you hadn't you'd be dead," he shot back.

Neither wanted to admit that the other was right.

Eventually, I was released from the hospital and ordered a car to go home, forced to lean forward in the passenger seat because it was too painful to lean back.

I returned to work after a few days and had to explain in detail the reasons behind my unexpected leave of absence. Each detail felt like yet another pinprick in the trial balloon of my attempt to earn the leadership role of the department.

Pat Faber eventually set up a meeting for early Tuesday morning. We terminated people on Tuesdays so the selection of this day caused me concern. He greeted me without his usual banter and somberly waved me over to a seat in his office. He waited a moment to collect his thoughts. In that time I scanned the shelves behind him. They, too, were lined with crystal trophies and awards just as Bob Gershon's shelves had been. I wondered if they were legitimate.

The firm would never terminate me because I lost the bid to take the leadership role, but they would make it clear that my future there was not a long-term option. I would scuffle along for a few years and then quietly be forced out. But I was too young to retire and would have to reinvent myself with all the youthful energy and drive it takes to reestablish a career. That thought made me sick to my stomach.

"There's a stretch of country behind my house in Palm Desert," he began, and I thought to myself, this bastard has more houses than hairs on his head. I also pondered the fact that I had heard every single one of Pat's folksy metaphors but I had never heard this one. "It's named after an old prospector who tried to make his fortune in the hills. There are still remnants of his work—old wash sluice boxes, pickaxes, tunnels carved out of the scrabble. I take Bessie back there and let her run. She loves the open country, as do I."

"Me, too," I think I muttered, but Pat ignored me. He even looked a little miffed that I was interfering with his rhythm.

"There's one cave in particular back there," he began again. "Bessie stumbled upon it. It's up a narrow canyon that I'm sure no one has seen except for the man who made it. And me." There was a thick vein of pride in his voice. "The front is collapsed, the beams forming a big X, but you can see somewhat in there, depending on the time of day. If you shout inside it takes a long time for your echo to come back. It's deep. I can't tell you how many times I have stood in front of that cave. Bessie, the old girl, she won't go near it. It scares her. It intrigues her but it scares her. At some point in life, Chuck, a man is going to come upon a cave like this one."

My mind raced with the possibilities of what the cave stood for. Was it my career—abandoned, hopeless, a hole of lost dreams? Was it Pat's delusional self-journey—daring, solitary, the pinnacle of his life's work?

"And you have a decision to make. The hardest decision in your life because the cave has so many unknowns." My heart sank with each additional line. "Chuck, I stood there this past weekend and stared at that entrance for an hour. And a single thought came to me.

"A black rock isn't black in the dark," he stated, and paused long enough for those profound words to sink in. I found myself nodding along with him despite not understanding anything that was coming out of his mouth.

"Chuck, you are the man to lead this group. Congratulations," he said and rose to shake my hand.

I rose to accept with a handshake and squeezed harder than I needed to. "Pat, I know this wasn't an easy decision," I told him. He brushed it off but I could tell he was very proud of the "courage" he exhibited in selecting me. "You made the right decision."

Not one to miss an opportunity to cut someone

down a peg, he shot back, "Then you have your mission. Prove it to me."

We chatted a little bit further about the group and the direction in which it needed to go, but he had no time for petty details. His work was done and it was time to get another coffee. At the door, I turned back to ask the question that was gnawing at me.

"Hey Pat, if you don't mind telling me, what was it that made you go with me?"

He thought about it a moment, then said, "You were very honest in your interview."

The truth would be revealed some time later when I discovered the real reason I got the job. It had nothing to do with any answer in the interview, but everything to do with a few well-placed telephone calls by Carl Valenti to a few select, influential men at the firm. But I wasn't disappointed in the least. I had always believed that career success was driven by ten percent skill and ninety percent luck. I would forever be grateful for the opportunity to enter into that rarified air of upper management where one's entire role was just to be—to be and to give opinion.

My old boss Bob Gershon questioned this foundation but that was his biggest mistake. He searched for value, for meaning in the role. The value was simply having the role in the first place.

Later that day I got Paul's concession speech. He came into my office and gushed on and on about how happy he was for me, but I didn't believe it for a second. I would in time hear about how Paul had done everything in his power to discredit me with anyone who would listen during the run-up to the interviews.

This was revealed to me on numerous occasions after I got the promotion. It was standard corporate operating procedure to curry favor with the new lead by bad-mouthing the guy who had bad-mouthed me.

But I was the victor and needed to display a modicum of humility and to rise above it all and be the better man; righteousness came easily when I had all the power. I put out my hand and Paul, in typical Paul fashion, took hold of it and pulled me in close for a big man-hug. He slapped me hard on my back, too hard, and I winced from the still lingering pain from the hammer blows.

"Paul, let's meet next week to discuss the obesity campaign," I offered as an olive branch. Paul accepted it enthusiastically and rattled off several new ideas on how to make it a success. I just smiled to myself because I knew that my very first decision as head of the group was to cancel all work on the campaign. Paul's rabid pursuit of anyone over 150 pounds would finally come to an end, and the one great accomplishment of my career would be what I chose not to carry out.

I had other designs for Paul. And decorum be damned, I was going to make his life a living hell. His first job for me was to make a recommendation on whether we should renew the contract with Badger as our lead investigator. I would let him do the due diligence he needed to discover all of the unseemly details about Badger. I would let him passionately recommend that we terminate relations with him and his firm. And I would wait until the very end before I overruled him without even the slightest of reasons why. Badger was someone I wanted around.

No one wanted Sami Halilayen around. He was convicted of the murder of Morgan McIlroy and sentenced to life. Police easily pieced together the events that led to her being strangled in the backseat of her own car, and it ended up being a fast trial. Morgan was one of Sami's many conquests, one of several involving underage girls. Upon learning about his relationship with Jeanette, Morgan confronted him in a meeting at the parking lot in Chinatown. Her prospective disclosures threatened to dismantle whatever fragile spiritual empire he was building, never mind the specter of landing in state prison for statutory rape, and for that she had to be killed.

There never was any link between Sami and Tala's activities to extort money. As far as the police were concerned, they were separate incidents. There were surprisingly few details about Morgan's murder in the press and no charges were ever filed for the illegal acts Sami performed on underage girls, one of which resulted in a baby boy. For once the influence of the powerful resulted in a good outcome—it was better for all involved if the past remained in the past.

As for Valenti and the others, it became clear that they didn't want me around much either. I tried several times to connect with the Valenti clan, but all of my feelers went unanswered. It felt like a nonverbal dismissal. I instead followed their lives from afar through the press.

The museum plan for the edge of Chinatown was scratched in favor of a different spot farther up the hill in the Alpine District. It was another random spot but maybe not as random as it looked on the surface. Gao Li was back in the fold as he and Valenti formed a partnership to develop the area into a mixed-use space with the museum serving as the cultural centerpiece. Valenti had seized upon the opportunity with his granddaughter in the birthing clinic to knock Gao off his perch. But they were each man enough to put their differences aside when this new opportunity arose— money once again proved to be the great unifier. There they were on TV praising each other's virtues as they unveiled the elaborate design for the new museum. Valenti had hired a new architect who clearly understood his vision and the need for that third story with his name emblazoned across the top.

Also back in the fold was the hapless Jeff Schwartzman. He was there during all of the ceremonies but you sort of had to look for him back among the throngs of people. He was the one smiling the most. Valenti had pardoned him for past sins and granted him that which he wanted all along—directorship of the museum. He had the title but it was unclear if any power came with it. I had the sense Jeff only wanted the title.

It was too late to remove the ballot initiative that was at the heart of the museum conflict. As autumn fell over the city, voters went to the polls and overwhelmingly endorsed a measure they didn't understand. Some bright developer would eventually exploit this unwanted measure in the years to come, but for now it was just a bunch of meaningless words etched forever in the books of this great city.

With autumn came the bright days and cooler nights, and my desire for central air conditioning dissipated but not my desire for the hundred grand that I was supposed to use to install it. The raise I'd just gotten with my promotion could finance the AC, but that didn't tamp down my aggravation with Valenti for stiffing me on the payment. Perhaps he thought saving my job was enough of a reward, but I never would have needed that help if I hadn't gotten involved with him in the first place. I let my anger fester until one Saturday I decided to confront him. I drove out to Benedict Canyon and parked my car in front of the Valenti compound. I waited most of the day before the front gate. I convinced myself that I needed that money but inside I knew it was for other reasons.

Late in the afternoon the front gate swung open, and I saw the black sedan coming down the driveway. I got out of my car and stood in the middle of the entrance to block it from leaving. The sedan slowed to a stop. Hector was at the wheel. He stared at me from behind dark glasses. I could see the white-haired gentleman in the backseat. I went around to the side of the sedan, the rear window rolled down, and Valenti stuck his head out.

"Let me guess," he smiled, "you want your money."

"Fuck off," I told him. "I want to talk to Hector." There was a long, awkward pause. "Alone," I said.

Eventually the rear door opened and the old man dragged himself out. I watched him take the long walk back toward the house, and that moment was worth far more than any hundred thousand dollars.

Hector got out of the front seat and shook his head but I could tell that even he enjoyed it. Despite the ordeal he had gone through, he didn't look any different. Black shoe polish really was the great concealer. I didn't know what to say to him so I just put out my hand and settled on, "Thank you."

"What for?"

"For saving my life," I told him. "I guess I owe you."

At which point he tossed my hand aside like it was something rotten.

"You don't owe me shit," he said. That same logic had changed the course of his life and he didn't want it to change mine.

A car desperately in need of a new muffler coughed its way toward us. I recognized Nelson at the wheel and moved out of the way to let him pass. As the car went by I spied Jeanette in the backseat with the baby. Whether it was deliberate or not, she didn't look up. Perhaps it was better that way—the last thing she would need was any kind of reminder of the events that led her to that moment. But for me, just getting a glimpse of her put my own mind at ease. As the clunker rattled up the driveway I turned back to Hector.

"She living here now?" Hector nodded. "The old man must be in all his glory." Hector didn't have to confirm it because I was certain that was the case. I could even see it on the old man's face when I told him to leave us to talk.

We stood there for a moment but there was really nothing left to say and it was slowly becoming uncomfortable, so I just wished him goodbye and headed back to my car.

I drove along the ridgeline until I came to one of the passes. I made the turn and crested the top of the hill and then began the long, rapid descent toward the Westside.

There were questions that needed to be answered.

☺ ☺ ☺

The details surrounding the blackmailing scheme defied logic. The first request for money came from Jeanette for $45,000. I assumed that money was for the payment to the birthing clinic. She had asked Morgan for a similar amount. The money was paid to Nelson's brother who was clearly doing his little sibling a favor by collecting it in case there was trouble.

Nothing after that made sense.

Jeanette had the baby in the dingy clinic in Alhambra but was kicked out after Gao got a call from an anonymous woman alerting him to her location. If the caller's goal was money, she could have easily extorted it from Gao but she never asked for it. Then Jeanette inexplicably leaked her own story to a gossip blogger. I assumed this was her way of putting pressure on Valenti to ramp up the price of her return. But when I spoke to the kids at Nelson's house, they kept talking about some minuscule amount of money—fifty grand—when the amount requested and delivered to Tala was in the millions. That was where the anonymous female caller returned, and this time it couldn't have been Tala. Someone had tipped Sami off to Jeanette's location at the Beverlywood house. Someone wanted her and the baby dead.

Meredith answered the door. Maybe it was the weather but this time she wore a plain pair of jeans and a loose-fitting cardigan. You couldn't be impressed by the lack of body fat under that ensemble. There was a change in attitude as well. Gone was the transparent pursuit of attention under the overly flirtatious behavior, which only succeeded in making you feel sorry for her. She just looked like a pretty, middle-aged woman who shopped at one of the higher-end department stores. Meredith led me into the living room and we sat in chairs facing each other.

"I'd pay you the money if I had it," she said.

"I know you would," I told her. "But that's not why I am here. Have you spoken to her?"

"Have you?" Meredith asked hopefully, and I correctly assumed she hadn't. I shook my head. "Jeanette's living with Dad now."

"I just came from there." Despite informing her that Jeanette and I hadn't spoken, she leaned in as if I were about to give an update, but I had very little to give. "She looks good. Nelson seems to still be in the picture."

"That's good," she said. "Poor kid will eventually realize he's gay but for now it's better for both of them to have each other. She'll need that support. And Dad?"

I hadn't realized the extent of her exile.

"I don't know, it's always hard to tell with him," I started. "He seems happy."

"I'm sure. It's a second chance for him."

I heard no resentment in her words. I gathered from previous talks with Meredith and from my own observations that the old man wasn't the best father out there. And it seemed that Meredith was coming to the same ugly conclusion about her own efforts. Behind the "second chance" was a hope that there would be one for her. She conveyed that in an odd, but brutally honest way.

"The truly unforgivable is to fail as a parent," she said.

Once again I was treading in a world I knew nothing about. But I refused to believe in that kind of finality.

"Nothing is unforgivable," I told her. "It might just take a very long time."

My words warmed her more than I intended. We talked for a little while about nothing in particular. Soon she slipped back into staring out the sliding door at the expanse on the other side of the glass, and I slipped out the front door without saying goodbye.

My suspicion that Meredith was the anonymous caller no longer felt plausible. She may have inadvertently put her daughter in danger allowing a man like Sami into their household. She may have ignored some of the early signs that Jeanette needed help. She may have done a lot of things that were now coming back to haunt her as only regret can. But I just couldn't believe she willfully wanted her daughter dead.

That left only one other person.

AN ENDLESS SUNSET

I arrived at the convalescent home after visiting hours. The front desk was empty and I proceeded down the main hallway. I glanced inside the little chapel with the dimly lit, makeshift altar but didn't expect to find her there. I went up the stairs and stepped out onto the balcony. The taillights from outbound traffic cast the entire area in a reddish glow. A voice called out to me.

"I'm over here," the old woman said.

Sheila Lansing sat in the same chair under the potted palm and looked out at the passing traffic like she was watching a beautiful sunset from a quiet beach, except this kind of sunset never ended.

"What do you want?" she asked as I stood over her.

"I want to know why."

"You know why."

"I want you to say it."

Sheila fixed her gaze on the void in front of her. I needed her to look at me, to acknowledge my presence, so I moved to my right and cast her face in shadow.

"Because he ruined my life," replied the voice from the dark.

"Are you aware of what you did?" I asked. "Two people lost their lives. One of them was just a young girl."

"I didn't have anything to do with—"

"Neither of them deserved it," I cut in. I couldn't let her slough off Morgan's murder. Without the old woman's meddling, that girl would be breathing today. I then thought of the Sunday morning that almost got me killed and what the scene could have looked like in that little house if Sami had been successful. I felt something I had never experienced before—a desire to inflict harm on another human being.

"Did you think three million dollars would hurt him?" I asked. "Three *billion* dollars wouldn't hurt him."

"It wasn't about the money," she dismissed.

"Then why the ransom?"

"So we could get out of here."

Sheila clarified the "we" for me—it included her, Jeanette, and the baby. She admitted that the chance encounter with Jeanette wasn't entirely that. She helped orchestrate the program with Jeanette's school. And how elated she was when she finally got to meet the young woman. "She is such a sweet girl," she said without any acknowledgment of how odd it sounded coming from her. "She listened to me. She cared for me. And I cared for her."

When Sheila found out that Jeanette was pregnant, she and Tala helped get her into the clinic in Alhambra. "You know he turned his back on her when he found out she was pregnant," she said like an accusation directed at me. "A grandparent doesn't do that." That was her one triumph over Valenti—a feeling of superiority in one aspect of life.

Now they had a baby boy and the scheme was cooked up to bleed money out of Valenti so they could all run off together. Her plan was as harebrained as the one Jeanette and Nelson pitched me. I guessed their "home" would be the old one she'd been forced to leave in Pacoima, but when I asked her where she intended to go, she answered, "Anywhere but here."

The fantasy life she projected didn't feel genuine. The words were right but the weight behind them was missing. I felt no love for a young girl or her baby. There was only anger.

"Why did you try to have them killed, Mrs. Lansing?" I stared down at the face in shadow but could glean nothing. "You hate him that much?"

"It's more than just hate," she whispered.

Sheila tugged at the quilt protecting her from the cool night air. Even in the shadow I could see how thin and brittle her arms were.

"What a great man, with all his success and money and charity," she said. "The same man who, when he found out I couldn't have children, tossed me aside like an old dish towel. After all I did for him. The way he looked at me," she stammered back to some memory from decades past. "At least an old rag has some use.

"Poor Charlie," she said, "he tried so hard." It took me a moment to realize her mind had leapfrogged in time to a second marriage and more precious memories that unfortunately weren't quite precious enough. She shook her head at that sad realization and was jerked back to the memory that haunted her.

"I knew on that day the only thing Carl cared more about, even more than money, was having a child." A measure of control returned to her voice. "And that one day I would take from him what he took from me."

"Jeanette is living with him now," I told her. "By her own choice. She's happy."

I had the urge to cause her pain and those two sentences were the best way to do it. I couldn't see her face but I knew they had their intended effect. But even though I held nothing but contempt for the woman whose phone calls from this nursing home—the heads-up to Gao, the demand for three million, the tip-off to Sami—cascaded a series of events that led to so much suffering, I didn't feel good about the way I told her about Jeanette and the baby. The words came out too easily for my liking. A second urge overcame me, and that was to get away from this place as soon as possible.

I stepped back and her face was again illuminated by the outbound traffic. She stared as if hypnotized by the red lights. I looked at her exposed arms, thinner than I ever thought arms could be. I felt cold just looking at her.

I took up the quilt and wrapped it around her shoulders, then left her alone on the balcony to join my own set of taillights, heading in the opposite direction.

About the Author

Adam Walker Phillips is the author of *The Silent Second*, as well as an executive at a global financial services company who has endured countless Power-Point decks, offsite visioning sessions, synergies, and synergistically minded cross-functional teams, all in service of his work as a novelist to tell the story of an HR man–turned–moonlighting detective. He holds an MFA in film from Columbia University, and lives in the Eagle Rock neighborhood of Los Angeles with his wife and children.